A KISS OF LOVE

Then Malvina found herself pondering as she had before she fell asleep of the kiss the Duc had given her in the hall.

She had never been kissed before, although quite a number of men had tried to do so, either in the gardens of Devonshire House or in some empty reception room when she was attending a private ball.

She had always believed that a kiss was a sensation too intimate to be wasted on a man who meant nothing to her.

Now she told herself that she would never see the Duc again –

Yet she had the uncomfortable feeling it would be impossible to forget his kiss.

It had not been what she expected.

Nor had she thought that she herself would feel like responding to him.

Yet when his lips did touch hers, she felt a strange feeling she had never felt before move through her breasts.

Even as she had become aware of it, he had left her. He had just walked out of the door without looking back.

Only when she was lying in bed and could not sleep did she feel again that strange unaccountable feeling.

She wanted to tell herself it was what everyone felt when they were first kissed.

THE BARBARA CARTLAND PINK COLLECTION

Titles in this series

A KISS OF LOVE

BARBARA CARTLAND

Barbaracartland.com Ltd

THE BARBARA CARTLAND PINK COLLECTION

Barbara Cartland was the most prolific bestselling author in the history of the world. She was frequently in the Guinness Book of Records for writing more books in a year than any other living author. In fact her most amazing literary feat was when her publishers asked for more Barbara Cartland romances, she doubled her output from 10 books a year to over 20 books a year, when she was 77.

She went on writing continuously at this rate for 20 years and wrote her last book at the age of 97, thus completing 400 books between the ages of 77 and 97.

Her publishers finally could not keep up with this phenomenal output, so at her death she left 160 unpublished manuscripts, something again that no other author has ever achieved.

Now the exciting news is that these 160 original unpublished Barbara Cartland books are already being published and by Barbaracartland.com exclusively on the internet, as the international web is the best possible way of reaching so many Barbara Cartland readers around the world.

The 160 books are published monthly and will be numbered in sequence.

The series is called the Pink Collection as a tribute to Barbara Cartland whose favourite colour was pink and it became very much her trademark over the years.

The Barbara Cartland Pink Collection is published only on the internet. Log on to www.barbaracartland.com to find out how you can purchase the books monthly as they are published, and take out a subscription that will ensure that all subsequent editions are delivered to you by mail order to your home.

NEW

Barbaracartland.com is proud to announce the publication of ten new Audio Books for the first time as CDs. They are favourite Barbara Cartland stories read by well-known actors and actresses and each story extends to 4 or 5 CDs. The Audio Books are as follows:

The Patient Bridegroom	The Passion and the Flower
A Challenge of Hearts	Little White Doves of Love
A Train to Love	The Prince and the Pekinese
The Unbroken Dream	A King in Love
The Cruel Count	A Sign of Love

More Audio Books will be published in the future and the above titles can be purchased by logging on to the website www.barbaracartland.com or please write to the address below.

If you do not have access to a computer, you can write for information about the Barbara Cartland Pink Collection and the Barbara Cartland Audio Books to the following address:

Barbara Cartland.com Ltd., Camfield Place,
Hatfield, Hertfordshire AL9 6JE, United Kingdom.
Telephone: +44 (0)1707 642629
Fax: +44 (0)1707 663041

THE LATE DAME BARBARA CARTLAND

Barbara Cartland who sadly died in May 2000 at the age of nearly 99 was the world's most famous romantic novelist who wrote 723 books in her lifetime with worldwide sales of over 1 billion copies and her books were translated into 36 different languages.

As well as romantic novels, she wrote historical biographies, 6 autobiographies, theatrical plays, books of advice on life, love, vitamins and cookery. She also found time to be a political speaker and television and radio personality.

She wrote her first book at the age of 21 and this was called *Jigsaw*. It became an immediate bestseller and sold 100,000 copies in hardback and was translated into 6 different languages. She wrote continuously throughout her life, writing bestsellers for an astonishing 76 years. Her books have always been immensely popular in the United States, where in 1976 her current books were at numbers 1 & 2 in the B. Dalton bestsellers list, a feat never achieved before or since by any author.

Barbara Cartland became a legend in her own lifetime and will be best remembered for her wonderful romantic novels, so loved by her millions of readers throughout the world.

Her books will always be treasured for their moral message, her pure and innocent heroines, her good looking and dashing heroes and above all her belief that the power of love is more important than anything else in everyone's life.

"A kiss between a man and a woman in love is the deepest and most sincere expression of feeling that human beings can aspire to."

Barbara Cartland

CHAPTER ONE
1878

Lady Malvina Silisley ran downstairs as she heard the horses come to a standstill outside the front door.

Her father, the Earl of Silstone, stepped out from his carriage just as she reached him.

She flung her arms round his neck.

"You are back, Papa! I have missed you so much. How could you stay away for so long?"

"It was only a week, my dearest," he replied, "but I am flattered that you found it lonely without me."

"Very very lonely, Papa, but I have lots to tell you, so come in and have your tea. It is waiting for you in the drawing room."

They walked into the impressive mansion that had been the home of the Earls of Silstone for three centuries.

It had, however, fallen into considerable disrepair before her father, the fifth Earl, had inherited the estate.

He had been lucky enough to inherit a huge fortune from a Godfather who had gone exploring the world and finally, before he died, touched gold.

The Silisleys had always regretted that the head of their family could not live in the big house, so there was general rejoicing when the Earl started to restore it.

He was ably assisted by his wife who fortunately had exquisite taste.

The result when they had completed the restoration was to turn Silstone Court into one of the most beautiful ancestral homes in the entire country.

The Earl was welcomed in the neighbourhood – not just for his wealth but for himself.

He was an extremely genial gentleman, charming and good-tempered and ready to help anyone he met.

As soon as he came into such a large fortune he had assisted quite a number of his contemporaries.

He was, in fact, ready to listen to any story of hard luck that was told to him.

He was blissfully happy with his Countess until she died and he adored his very attractive daughter.

The only sadness was that he had no son to inherit the title and estates.

All would go, on the Earl's death, to a rather boring cousin whom no one particularly liked.

However, the Earl was still comparatively young.

People often whispered that he was likely to marry again and produce the much wanted heir.

In the meantime he was very busy.

His daughter, Malvina, had just left school after an extensive and a very expensive education.

She had ended up in the most renowned Finishing School for girls in St. Cloud just outside Paris.

The school was kept by nuns and was attached to a Convent.

The pupils all came from the aristocracies of every European country and the most experienced teachers and masters in France were employed by the school.

Malvina had returned home with flying colours.

Her report was exceptionally good and she had four distinctions and prizes to prove it.

She was thrilled to be home.

During her father's recent absence she had spent the time riding his fine horses and exploring what had been added to the house since she had been away.

She was particularly attracted to the library and it was a delight to her that her father had bought all the recent books that had just been published in London.

Now as she went with her father into the house, she was talking about the mares that had just foaled and the orchids that had just come into bloom.

These were a new possession and had been brought to them from the East.

"You must come with me and see these wonderful orchids, Papa, as soon as we have finished tea," enthused Malvina when they reached the drawing room.

It was a particularly attractive room, having been furnished by the late Countess with furniture of the Louis XIV period.

The pictures were by famous French artists, many of which had been purchased by the Earl in France when they came to visit Malvina at her Finishing School.

As the Countess had always demanded, there was a profusion of flowers everywhere.

The bright sunshine streaming through the windows glittered on the beautiful silver standing on the tea-table.

"Now I have told you all my news," Malvina said, as she passed her father the hot scones, "tell me what you have been doing in London."

There was a slight pause before the Earl responded,

"I have been finding you a husband, my dearest – "

Malvina's large and beautiful eyes opened wide.

She stared at her father as if she thought she must have misheard him.

"*Husband!*" she repeated after a pause.

"I have been worried, my very precious daughter, because when we travel to London for the Season and open the house in Park Lane, you will be certainly be pursued by every fortune-hunter in London."

Malvina laughed.

"You need not worry, Papa, I am too intelligent to be deceived by a man who desires my money rather than me."

"Because you are so beautiful, Malvina, you will undoubtedly be desired for yourself, but there is always the cream sitting on the top of the cake which is that you are also exceedingly rich."

"I never, for a moment, think about my money," murmured Malvina.

"I know that, dearest, but those who meet you will certainly talk about it. I know those fortune-hunters only too well and how clever they can be in deceiving a pretty woman into believing it is only love that counts."

"I cannot think why you are worrying about it now, Papa. I am not going to get married and leave you. I have been away far too long and it is Heaven to be home again."

Her father looked at her with loving eyes.

"That is what I want you to feel. At the same time I think I have found the perfect husband for you and there will be no need for you to look any further."

There was silence until Malvina spoke up,

"Are you *really* serious about this, Papa?"

"Very serious, my dearest."

"Do you really think that I could marry a man I have never met and whom I don't know?" Malvina asked him.

"It is nothing like that," the Earl answered. "The husband I have chosen for you is someone you have heard of,

4

even if you have not actually met him since you were a child. He is a charming and delightful young man and I just know instinctively that you will be exceedingly happy together."

"I think, Papa, that it is for me to decide. But tell me about this man who has made such a good impression on you."

The Earl sat back in his chair.

"You will be surprised, Malvina, when I tell you that he is actually our next door neighbour. In fact a great advantage of your marriage to him will be that sooner or later we will be able to join up our estates, and make it one of the most outstanding and admirably managed in the whole of England."

"I don't know what you are talking about, Papa, in fact I am trying to remember who our next door neighbour is."

"I suppose because you have been abroad for so long being educated, you will have forgotten that it is the Marquis of Arramford, who lives only a few miles away and whose estate meets ours by the River Need."

"Oh, I think I remember now."

"I met the Marquis at White's Club only three days ago," the Earl continued, "and he told me how worried he is that his son, who is the Earl of Arram, shows no sign of getting married. He is approaching twenty-seven and the Marquis feels that by this time he should have settled down and started a family.

"As your mother and I were, the Marquis is very anxious for his son to have an heir. Otherwise, if anything happens to Charles, the Marquisate might become extinct as apparently they have very few relations left."

"It all sounds most complicated," sighed Malvina. "But if Charles Arram does not wish to get married, I do not see what anyone, least of all I, can do about it."

The Earl chuckled.

"He *will* marry you and his father thinks it is a most excellent idea. He is overjoyed. Not only because you are my daughter and he has always been a great friend of mine, but also, like a great many Noblemen at the moment, he is feeling the pinch.

"He needs money for his house and for his estate. Nothing would give him greater pleasure than to have you as his daughter-in-law."

"What you are really telling me, Papa, is that he is *fortune-hunting*!"

"Of course he is. Every father with a handsome son to inherit his title wants him to marry someone he loves and who is very beautiful, but who also has a large dowry to keep the old place going."

Malvina did not speak.

"The same does apply, as you would know only too well, when ambitious mothers look for someone with a title to marry their daughters."

He gave a laugh before he added,

"Of course I am ambitious for you, my dearest, but short of marrying Royalty, I would be very delighted to see you the wife of a young man who will eventually be the Marquis of Arramford."

"If you ask me," Malvina said after a moment, "it all sounds slightly unpleasant. I used to talk to the girls at school about love and we all wanted to meet a charming, handsome man who would fall in love with us and whom we, in return, would love with all our heart."

"That is exactly what will happen. I am only saving you from being courted by all the rag-tag and bob-tail of London simply because you are rich. Charles Arram has as much to offer you as you have to offer him."

He waited for Malvina to say something, but when she remained silent, he carried on,

"Their family is far older than ours and the Marquis has a very distinguished position at Court. In fact Queen Victoria is very fond of him and would like to have him with her for more time than he can spare from his estate."

"So just what have you arranged?" Malvina asked in a hard voice.

She was feeling both horrified and shocked at what her father was saying to her.

She knew him too well to protest immediately yet she told herself that she had no intention of marrying a man whose father desired her money or a suitor whom her own father chose for her without any consultation.

However, she was too intelligent to say much until she had discovered the whole story.

In a voice which she deliberately kept under control she remarked,

"I feel rather bewildered, Papa. Tell me the story from the very beginning. You met the Marquis at White's and so he confided in you, because people always tell you their troubles, that he was worried about his son."

"That is more or less true," he admitted. "I asked him how Charles was doing and he said he was enjoying himself as most young men do. But he thought it was time he settled down."

"Why should he think that?"

Her father smiled.

"Well you know or you must have heard what most young men are like. The flowers are there for the picking, and they would be stupid if they refused to enjoy them."

"What you are saying, Papa, is that Charles Arram has had a lot of love affairs?" Malvina asked sharply.

"Of course, as any man has when he is turned loose in the Social world and is welcomed with open arms."

"Then why has he not married?"

"Because, my dearest, his *affaires-de-coeur*, as the French always put it, have always been with women who are already tied to another man or perhaps widowed."

He paused.

"There has been no talk nor gossip about Charles getting married. I gather, being young and handsome, he has played the field, so to speak."

"Do you think it has begun to bore him?" Malvina enquired. "Or has his father just made up his mind that he should take life more seriously?"

The Earl gave his daughter a quick glance.

He thought that her questions were intelligent and she was behaving very calmly.

He had expected she might be somewhat hysterical and refuse even to discuss an arranged marriage.

Instead she was questioning him in a manner that he had to admire.

Aloud he resumed,

"The Marquis told me that Charles is at present in Paris. I have arranged that, when he returns, his father will bring him over to luncheon or dinner. We are both quite certain that when you meet each other, you will both find everything will fall into place."

"I think, Papa, you are backing an outsider. From all that I have read, although as you know I have had no personal experience, love comes to one unexpectedly and not usually where it is required."

The Earl laughed.

"You have been reading too many novels, my dear.

I can assure you it is very easy for a young man to fall in love with a very beautiful young woman, and that is what you are."

"And Charles Arram?"

"His father tells me women have pursued him ever since he left the cradle. He is exceedingly good-looking and enjoys life in a way that makes those with him enjoy it too."

There was silence again and then Malvina asked,

"What is he doing in Paris at the moment?"

"Need you ask that question, even though you have not seen the part of Paris he is frequenting. You must have heard even in your Convent that it is the most glamorous spot in the whole of Europe. The beauty, wit and charm of their women are universally acclaimed."

The Earl sighed.

"When I hear what goes on in Paris, I so often wish I was a young man again – "

"You are not yet old, Papa. Why not go to Paris and enjoy yourself?"

"To be honest I would rather be at home with you, and that reminds me, I have to go North next week."

"Oh, no, Papa! Why?"

"I have received a letter from my factor telling me of urgent repairs which are very badly needed at the Castle. He also suggests that I might be able to purchase several hundred acres of moorland just to the North of our Scottish estate."

"I should have thought our moors are large enough already."

"I could always do with a little extra," he replied. "The owner of these moors, which are extremely good for grouse-shooting, has just died."

"So you think that you had better go and see them, Papa?"

"I will not be away for long. Ten days at the most. Then afterwards we will go up to London. I know that we should have gone earlier, but you have only just returned from your school.

"In fact I think if we have the whole of June there, which, of course, includes Royal Ascot, we shall have had enough festivities and be glad to return to the country."

"What you are really saying, Papa, is that you want me to be involved, if that is the right word, with Charles Arram before we go to London."

The Earl smiled.

"If you are engaged, even secretly, to Charles, there will be no need to bore ourselves with *debutantes* of the same age as you. With your looks and brains it will save giving endless luncheons and dinners to ambitious Mamas, who hope that you will fancy their sons who have empty pockets and, as far as I am concerned, empty heads!"

Malvina giggled.

"You are so funny, Papa, when you talk like that. At the same time I can see you scheming to get your own way!"

"Of course I want my own way," the Earl admitted. "And I feel nothing could be happier for all of us than to be united with the Arramford family."

Malvina did not answer.

Her father had just arrived home and she did not want to quarrel with him immediately on his arrival.

Also she knew him so well.

She was aware he had already made up his mind on this marriage, and it was going to be difficult to persuade him the match was something she personally did not want under any circumstances.

Later when she went upstairs to dress for dinner she asked herself,

'How can I possibly fall in love with any man who has been chosen for me by my father?'

Her bath had already been arranged in front of the fireplace with the hot and cold water carried up the stairs by the footmen.

The housemaids poured the water into the bath and scented it with oil of violets.

As Malvina climbed into it, she was thinking how comfortable she was at home.

She had no wish to go elsewhere.

'I am only eighteen,' she said to herself. 'Why on earth should I be married off, as if Papa was afraid I should end up on the shelf as an old maid?'

She was fully aware that this was not the reason.

Her father had always been ambitious.

He had been poor when he was a boy before he had inherited his great fortune and he still felt he was climbing the ladder towards success – so to satisfy himself he must gain more and more.

'Whatever Papa may say and whatever he may do,' thought Malvina as she bathed herself, 'I am not going to marry any man unless I love him with my heart and soul.'

The mere idea of her being rushed up the aisle for Charles Arram was horrifying, but she was too wise to say so to her father.

'I must now pretend,' she told herself, 'that I am agreeing to what Papa wants until I have seen Charles. If he turns out to be is as reluctant as I am, perhaps we can somehow persuade our parents to look elsewhere.'

Even as she thought of this strategy, she was aware that the Arramford family was in need of money.

Charles would therefore need it more than anyone else.

He was apparently living a life of gaiety amongst the most beautiful women of the *Beau Monde* and that was indisputably an expensive amusement.

Even more so if he was based in Paris.

Of course when at the Convent School the girls had talked about the *courtesans* who had made Paris so famous all over the world. Many of their brothers enjoyed the wit and beauty of the *cocottes*.

It would have been absurd for the pupils, however young and innocent, not to be aware of their considerable social importance in Paris.

There were stories of the extravagant parties given for them and of the jewellery and expensive flowers they received from their many admirers.

Their seductive beauty was whispered about in the dormitories after the girls had retired to bed.

"My brother was invited to a party," boasted one of Malvina's friends, "where in front of every girl there was a little bouquet with the stalks of the orchids each wrapped round with a thousand franc note!"

"A thousand francs," one girl exclaimed, "that must have been an expensive party!"

"There was a party," another girl piped up, "where Cora Pearl, whom every man finds so entrancing, danced a hornpipe on a floor covered in only white orchids."

Malvina felt at the time there was something cruel about such extravagance – she did not like to think of the beautiful orchids being crushed and thrown away without even being admired.

Other stories seemed so totally exaggerated and so extraordinary that she did not believe them.

At the same time it was impossible to live so near to Paris and not hear all about the strange goings-on of the *cocottes* and the gentlemen who pursued them.

'If I had a husband,' mused Malvina, 'I would very certainly not allow him to go to Paris without me!'

Then she remembered that Paris was where Charles Arram was at this moment.

'If that is what he enjoys, and apparently it is very enjoyable although expensive, he will certainly not wish to give it up when he is married.'

She found it difficult to sleep and when she did, she dreamt of beautiful women dancing on huge bouquets of flowers –

And of gentleman handing them endless banknotes of great value for doing so.

*

The next morning she and her Papa, as they usually did, rode for an hour before breakfast.

There was a private Racecourse beyond the stables and it was laid out with a section of jumps over which they took their horses.

Then they rode onto the flatter land and there they raced each other until both the horses and their riders were breathless.

"No one can ride as well as you do, Papa," Malvina enthused.

"The Marquis tells me his son is outstanding on a horse – "

Malvina was certain from the way he spoke and the reply coming so spontaneously, that he had been dwelling on her marriage, as indeed she had most of the night.

'I will not do it,' she told herself. 'But I shall not say so to Papa until the first excitement of the idea has died down.'

They had luncheon together and then Malvina took him round the greenhouses to see the special orchids which had just arrived from the East and also the other flowers with which they were experimenting.

The Earl was delighted with all he was shown and he promised he would make enquiries as to what other new flowers and plants were being brought to London.

"We are just so lucky, Papa, to have gardeners who enjoy flowers which are unusual and which require a great deal of attention."

"I agree with you, dearest, as you and I have always enjoyed anything unusual and out of the ordinary."

"Yes, Papa, and that is why I would enjoy meeting all different types of gentlemen before I would eventually even consider marrying anyone."

The Earl stiffened and then looked at his daughter in consternation.

"Are you suggesting giving me a foreigner as a son-in-law?" he asked.

"Why not, if he was something different from the ordinary Englishman for whom you have little respect?"

"That is nonsense, Malvina, of course I want you to marry an Englishman. As I have already told you, Charles is a perfect choice and you would be very stupid if you did not accept him."

"He has not asked me yet. Perhaps in Paris he is finding something more amusing than a wife."

"What on earth do you mean by that remark?" the Earl asked sternly.

"You know exactly what I mean. Although I have been at a Convent School, I am not entirely deaf or blind."

"I can see that it was a big mistake to send you to Paris, Malvina. Paris is for young men and who can blame them for enjoying it as I did many years ago."

He sighed before he continued more firmly,

"But you and I, my dearest one, are talking about marriage, which is a completely different matter. For that you need a *real* gentleman. A man whom you will respect. And the less you know about the world on the other side of the blanket, the better!"

Malvina laughed.

"Oh, Papa, this is an old-fashioned way of looking at things. And of course when I was in Paris I heard about the *cocottes*."

"That word should not pass your lips," the Earl said quickly.

"The girls talked about them and the newspapers we were allowed to see were full of the parties they had given and the huge sensation they had caused in the Bois de Boulogne."

She thought despite himself her father's eyes were twinkling.

"I also read of the enormous amount of jewellery the Parisian *cocottes* had received from Emperors, Kings and Princes – in fact from wealthy men of every nation."

"If I had known this sort of thing was going on, I would have brought you home immediately and sent you to a school in England," her father thundered.

"I have come to no harm, Papa. You cannot expect me not to enjoy hearing of other peoples' amusements even if they are not to my own taste."

"I should think not indeed! I am extremely annoyed that you should have learnt such things in what is supposed to be the finest Seminary for young ladies in the world."

"It is just unfortunate it is so near Paris," Malvina answered.

The Earl seemed troubled by this exchange.

Because she really loved her father, she went out of her way to make a fuss of him.

Malvina wanted to prevent him worrying over what she had just told him.

When her father suggested they should go over to Arramford Hall the following day, she accepted without making objections.

Anyway she thought it would be interesting to meet the Marquis and as his son was presently in Paris, she was not immediately faced with the problem of whether or not to accept him.

She was, however, well aware the next day that her father was showing her off.

He made a great fuss about what she was to wear and he was finally satisfied by a very pretty and expensive gown, which she had received from London soon after she arrived home.

The Earl drove her himself with his new team he had recently bought at Tattersalls – perfectly matched chestnut stallions.

As they sped along the lanes where the primroses were growing in the hedgerows they looked very romantic.

She did vaguely remember Arramford Hall as she had been invited there to children's parties when she was very young.

She had no memory at all of Charles, who, being eight years older, had not paid any attention to little girls.

The house was certainly imposing.

But as they drew nearer Malvina realised it needed a great many repairs. She could now understand even more clearly why the Marquis needed a rich daughter-in-law.

The carpets were worn, the covers of the sofas and chairs needed renewing.

A number of the pictures by several famous artists needed cleaning.

The Marquis, who was an extremely fine-looking gentleman, greeted them effusively.

"It is delightful to see you, Henry," he said to the Earl.

When he took Malvina's hand in his, he exclaimed,

"You are even more beautiful than your mother, whom I admired tremendously!"

"That is very flattering, my Lord," replied Malvina. "I only wish it was true."

"I can assure you that all the stories I have heard of your beauty are not exaggerated," added the Marquis.

He introduced her to some guests who were staying with him.

They were mostly relations – old and dreary, they had little of importance to say for themselves.

By the end of luncheon Malvina felt that she could understand why Charles Arram preferred Paris to being at home.

The Marquis paid her a great deal of attention and after they left the dining room, he insisted on taking her on a tour of the house.

She saw the Music room, the Ballroom, the Picture Gallery and the Adams Conservatory, as well as the State bedrooms, all in use for centuries.

Every room and all the contents needed attention to make them as perfect as they should be and Malvina was very conscious this was what her host was thinking.

She felt in a way she was sorry for him because he was going to be disappointed.

When they were alone for a moment because the

Earl had stopped to look closely at one particular picture, she ventured,

"I hear your son is living in Paris."

"Charles enjoys Paris. Unfortunately it is not only the most amusing place in France, but it is also the most expensive."

"That is what I heard when I was at school in St. Cloud," Malvina responded.

"It is just there for stupid young men to throw their money away," the Marquis said bitterly. "If I had my way I would have the whole City of Paris closed down!"

He spoke so sharply that Malvina was sure he was resenting every penny his son was spending.

Then because she thought it was a mistake to say any more, she changed the subject.

Driving home with her father, he asked tentatively,

"Tell me what do you think of Arramford Hall and of course its owner?"

She knew it was an important question for him.

"I thought the house was badly in need of repair – "

"I am sure with your taste, which is as good as your mother's, you will make it look as it should be."

When Malvina did not respond and after they had driven a little further, he remarked,

"I am sure that you liked the Marquis. He is a kind man and I have always been very fond of him."

"But you always do say nice things about everyone, Papa, whether they deserve it or not."

Her father gave her a quick glance.

"Are you hinting, Malvina, that you did not like the Marquis?"

"I thought he was over-eager to have your money to

spend on his house and had not made any effort on his own part to do anything about it."

Her father did not answer and they drove for nearly a mile without speaking.

Then as if to sum up what he was thinking silently, he countered,

"I feel sure you will think differently when Charles comes home."

"His father was most evasive as to when he would be expected," replied Malvina. "I heard you ask him twice and each time he did not answer."

The Earl said nothing more and they drove up to the front door.

Three footmen in their smart livery came hurrying down to open the carriage door.

"I always enjoy driving with you, Papa," Malvina sighed before she walked up the steps.

As she went upstairs to take off her hat, she knew that their visit to Arramford Hall had not been the success her father had hoped.

If her father had intended to impress her with what she would one day possess, he had made a grave mistake.

'If Charles Arram,' she pondered, 'is anything like his house, I have no wish to be friendly with him, let alone marry him. He is undoubtedly a bore!'

Then as she walked downstairs, she was wondering how she could convince her father.

First that his idea of joining the two estates together was just 'pie in the sky'.

Secondly that her marriage to Charles Arram would never become a reality.

*

The following morning at breakfast time there was a letter from Scotland.

It informed the Earl that the land he wanted to buy was coming onto the market sooner than he had expected.

His factor at Silstone Castle begged him to travel North immediately.

"There are quite a number of local gentlemen and farmers interested in the moors," he wrote, *"and if you're not here, my Lord, it will be easy to lose them.*

My opinion is that they'll greatly enhance the land Your Lordship already owns and should thus be a part of the Silstone estate."

The Earl read the letter to Malvina.

"I shall have to go North at once," he told her. "It is a nuisance, but as the sale will be earlier than expected, we may be able to go to London a week earlier."

"I am in no hurry," answered Malvina. "I am only sorry you have to go away so soon after my return."

"I am sorry too, my dearest. But you can easily go to one of our relations who would love to have you. There are plenty of them in the vicinity, as you know."

"I will think about it, Papa."

Her father's valet packed his clothes and the next morning he set off for London.

She knew he was being optimistic about how long his journey would take.

He decided the quickest way to reach their Castle in the North of Scotland would be by sea.

'There is not the slightest chance,' she told herself as she waved him goodbye, 'of his being back in less than two or three weeks.'

As she turned to walk into the house, she thought how lonely it would be without him.

Then she suddenly had an idea!

At first it seemed so astonishing and fantastic that she thought it was just nonsense.

She wandered into one of the beautifully furnished rooms where they often sat when they were alone.

Then she knew it was not only a possibility, but an adventure she had to undertake for her own protection.

What she really wanted was to see Charles Arram when he was not on his best behaviour – when he was not regarding her as a rich and acceptable bride.

He would then be off his guard and just himself.

'I will travel to Paris,' she decided, 'and see him. It should not be too difficult and if he really is as charming and wonderful as Papa believes he is, then when he returns home I can receive him very differently from the way I at first intended.'

It was something she knew she should not do and it would undoubtedly infuriate her father if he found out.

Equally she was fighting for her future happiness.

She could not be married to a man who had been allotted to her by two older men, who would benefit from her marriage and it was a situation she had no intention of accepting.

Yet she knew it was not going to be easy to fight her father.

Nor for that matter the Marquis.

She had seen by the expression in his eyes and the trouble he took in showing her over his house how much he wanted her as a member of his family.

It would be even more difficult, Malvina realised, to deal with her father.

He loved her and he firmly believed that what he was doing was the very best for her and her future.

He would in his own way produce every possible argument to make her, as he determined, see sense.

It would be very hard to resist him.

'I will have to provide him with proof,' Malvina told herself, 'that Charles is not the type of son-in-law he wants and least of all a man I should stoop to marry.'

She put her fingers up to her temple as she tried to work out her plan.

The difficulty was she had to hurry.

And she knew she could not travel alone to Paris.

A courier had always escorted her to and from her school together with a nun so that she would not encounter any difficulties on the journey.

'I must have someone with me,' she thought, 'and, of course, it *must* be Nanny.'

On the second floor there was the nursery that had become a schoolroom before Malvina had been sent to her Finishing School in Paris.

Nanny had always been there since she was a child and she still slept in the night nursery.

She had sat in the schoolroom when the Governess and Malvina were in other parts of the house.

Without thinking about it anymore, Malvina ran up the stairs to the nursery.

As she expected she found Nanny, although it was a warm day, sitting in front of the fire, knitting.

The items she knitted were distributed then among people in the village and because of her they had no excuse for ever contracting a cold or a sore throat – nor did they have to walk out when there was a sharp wind without a warm pullover.

When Malvina came into the room, Nanny looked up with a smile.

She was nearing her sixtieth birthday, but she still had the rosy cheeks and bright eyes Malvina remembered when she was still in the cradle.

"Oh, here you are then, Malvie," exclaimed Nanny. "I've been wondering when you would be coming to see your poor old Nanny!"

Nanny had always called her 'Malvie' ever since she was a little girl and could not pronounce her own name properly.

"I have not just come to see you, Nanny, but I want you to pack. Papa has gone away for at least a fortnight and we are going to London."

"Well, that'll be a big change. I suppose you've let them know at the house that you're coming."

"Yes, of course, Nanny, but I want to go in an hour or so. Will you pack your things at once?"

"There you are! I've been sitting here day after day, month after month, and then in you comes and gets the ball rolling."

"I know that you will enjoy it and when we get to London, we will decide where we will go next."

"I only hope it'll be to one of those houses that are comfortable," sighed Nanny. "The last time I stayed with your Aunt Ethel the draughts were something terrible and brought on my arthritis."

"We are not going to Aunt Ethel this time, Nanny. "But hurry because, as I said, I want to leave in an hour or so. We will be in London in time for dinner."

She did not wait to say any more as she knew that Nanny would be so delighted that something concrete was happening.

She often complained that since Malvina had had a Governess and then gone to school, there was nothing for her to do.

She was really indispensible in the house, but with no children to look after she had no acknowledged duties.

The other servants went their own way and did not always pay much attention to her.

Malvina was well aware that it would be a mistake to tell Nanny what she was planning before they left.

She would, of course, swear her to secrecy, but she might inadvertently reveal that they were actually going to Paris.

Her father's secretary would then doubtless think it his duty to inform the Earl where she had gone.

'I am not going to say a word to anyone until I am on my way,' Malvina decided.

She had already told her lady's maid that she might be staying with one of her relatives.

Some of her clothes were already packed when she reached her bedroom and she told the maid to put in some more dresses.

Then she thought that if she was in Paris, she would buy herself the clothes she intended to buy as a *debutante*.

Her father would be only too willing to pay for all of them, but what she wanted now was ready money with no questions asked.

She next changed into the clothes she was going to travel in and then she went to find her father's secretary.

Mr. Watkins was a most conscientious little man and he always wanted everything explained clearly to him.

"I have a great number of things to buy in London now I have left the Finishing School," Malvina told him. "And sometimes I will have to pay cash."

"It would be simpler, my Lady, to have all accounts sent to the house," replied Mr. Watkins.

"It's not simpler for me," retorted Malvina, "and I intend to visit shops where I am not known and it always takes time if one insists on opening an account."

She paused to let this sink in and then continued,

"What you can provide me with is a cheque book and I know Papa has already opened an account for me at the bank. I would like two hundred pounds in cash so that I need not immediately have to write out any cheques."

Against his best judgement, but finding it difficult to refuse Malvina, the secretary agreed.

She was given two hundred pounds, although he protested it was too much to put it in her handbag and also a cheque book which she had not taken with her to school.

She thanked him and as she was leaving the room, Mr. Watkins enquired,

"You have not given me the address where you will be going, my Lady. It is important that I should know where you will be staying."

"Yes, of course, Mr. Watkins. I shall be at Silstone House in Park Lane. Then I will let you know which of my relations will ask me to stay with them."

She felt that he was not satisfied with what she had told him, but slipped away before he could argue any more.

She and Nanny set off an hour-and-a-half later.

They were driven in the carriage that her father had driven from London with its team of fast horses.

There was a coachman and footman on the box and then her trunks were stacked behind.

There was plenty of room for the hat-boxes on the seat opposite where she and Nanny were sitting.

'This is such an adventure!' Malvina murmured to herself as they drove down the drive. 'Although Papa may be very angry with me, he will now be at sea and unable to prevent me from going to Paris!'

She was well aware that there could be difficulties ahead, but she thought that she would be incredibly stupid if she did not surmount them.

After all she knew Paris and if Nanny was with her as a chaperone no one could complain.

They drove out of the impressive lodge gates.

This was her answer to those who were determined to make her do whatever they wanted rather than what she desired.

'I have got to prove to them they are wrong before I can get my own way,' she thought. 'I mean not to have an arranged marriage, but to find eventually someone I will love and who will love me just for myself and not because I have so much money.'

CHAPTER TWO

Malvina and Nanny arrived in good time at Silstone House in Park Lane at three o'clock in the afternoon.

All the way Malvina was thinking out her plan for travelling to Paris.

She was very determined to see the man her father wanted her to marry without his being aware he was being observed.

They were greeted by the butler at Silstone House, who said somewhat reproachfully,

"We were not expecting your Ladyship here. His Lordship made no mention of your visit before he left."

"I had an invitation from one of my friends to come to London to a party she is giving, but I thought perhaps it would worry Papa when he had so much to think about, so I did not tell him what I was planning to do."

The butler smiled.

He had known Lady Malvina ever since she was born and he had spoilt her as soon as she could toddle with little tit-bits he kept in the pantry.

"Please tell cook, Bates, that we have already had luncheon, but Nanny and I would surely enjoy one of her special teas."

She knew this would please the old cook who had also been with the family for many years.

Then she ran upstairs to the room she always used.

There were a number of her dresses hanging in the wardrobe, but she did not reckon that any of them were smart enough to wear in Paris.

'I must go out to the shops tomorrow morning,' she concluded. 'And the sooner we leave for Paris the better.'

When she came downstairs she visited her father's other secretary who managed the house in London for him.

She told him much the same story that she had told the country secretary – that she wanted to buy some clothes in a hurry and did not wish to open any new accounts.

He protested strongly, as his counterpart had done, but eventually he did provide Malvina with three hundred pounds.

She concluded that now she had about enough to carry her through Paris and home again.

*

When she went shopping first thing in the morning, she put everything on account and did not spend a penny of the banknotes she had been given by the two secretaries.

She bought three dresses which were smart and up-to-date. They made her look older than the clothes she had worn at school.

The most important thing she had to do now was to find a courier to escort her and Nanny to Paris.

She knew where he was to be found and informed the manager of the agency who dealt with such bookings exactly what she wanted.

"You will understand," she explained firmly, "that he must meet us at Victoria Station, if you will now tell me the time of the morning train leaving for Dover. There will just be the two of us and our luggage."

The manager was impressed with her name and in the carriage that she had arrived in.

He promised her the best courier they had and one who had made the journey to Paris many times.

Malvina was determined that the courier should not come to Silstone House as he would undoubtedly tell Bates that she was going to Paris.

If he did and the secretary was told, the information would soon be conveyed to her father in Scotland.

'I must be very careful to cover all my tracks,' she determined.

When she went back to the house, she found Nanny comfortably arranged in one of the many sitting rooms.

She left her to climb upstairs to the attic as she had remembered on the way to London that her Aunt Beatrice had died five years ago at Silstone House.

Her belongings had all been taken up to the attics where a great number of family items had been stored over the years.

Aunt Beatrice had been a great beauty in her day. She had married Lord Morecambe who was a Secretary of State in the Government.

And it was on his death that she had come to live in Silstone House where she had entertained her many friends until she died.

Malvina remembered the trouble that she had taken to make herself look beautiful and graceful even when she was almost eighty.

She thought that among her aunt's belongings there would undoubtedly be some make-up that she might need to use herself when she reached Paris.

She was not mistaken.

There were a number of velvet and leather cases piled high on a table and they all bore her Aunt Beatrice's initials.

Malvina opened them one by one until she found what she was seeking.

It was a fairly large make-up box and it contained powder, rouge, mascara for the eyelashes and a pencil to draw the eyebrows.

Aunt Beatrice had always been very conscious of her appearance. No one ever saw her in the morning until she had tidied her hair and powdered her face.

Malvina now picked up the box and then she had another idea.

When her aunt was nearly seventy, she remembered she had disliked her hair going first grey and then white, so she therefore bought a wig in her natural colour. She had always worn it whenever she appeared in public.

Malvina recalled her mother laughing and saying,

"It was a very expensive wig but doubtless Beatrice will be able to save money on hairdressers!"

It took her some little time to find the wig, which had been put away in the bottom of the wardrobe.

It was in a beautifully packed box and the hair of the wig was not crushed nor the shape of it altered.

Malvina took it downstairs and placed it in a hat-box, putting on top of it the hats she was taking with her.

She thought if she unpacked the wig herself when they arrived, Nanny would not even know it existed.

'I do hope I have not forgotten anything,' she said to herself.

It was in fact Bates who reminded her that she was supposed to be going to a party.

"You'll be having dinner there no doubt, my Lady, and won't be requiring anything to eat this evening before you leave?"

Malvina was forced to use her brain swiftly.

"Oh, I forgot to tell you, Bates, the party has been postponed. It is very sad, but my friend for whom it was being given has developed a bad cold. Therefore everyone has been told that the party will take place on another day."

"I'm sorry to hear that, my Lady. Shall I tell cook you'll be in for dinner?"

"I would like a very light meal, please. Nanny and I are leaving tomorrow."

"So soon!" exclaimed Bates.

"I am going on to stay in the South of England with some friends. It is quicker to travel by train so a carriage must take us to the Railway Station at ten o'clock."

"I'll give the coachman his orders, my Lady, and I am sorry your visit to us is to be so short."

"There will be many more visits and you know that I am always happy here with you to look after me, Bates. But now I have left school I need to find again the friends I had in the past."

"I am sure that you'll find very many of them, my Lady," said Bates reassuringly. "Once his Lordship's back and you've come here for the Season, the invitations'll be rolling in."

Malvina thanked him profusely.

She enjoyed a simple but delicious dinner alone in the big dining room.

When she went up to bed, she looked again at her luggage.

She wanted to make certain that she had everything she would want in Paris.

But she was not quite certain what that would be.

*

They set off brightly the next morning with Bates bidding them 'God-speed'.

When they reached Victoria Station, Malvina found the courier who was waiting where she told him to wait – under the clock.

He already had First Class tickets in his hand for her and Nanny. He then escorted them to the train which was waiting to carry them to Dover.

It was only as they moved off that Nanny enquired,

"You've been doing things in such a hurry, Malvie, I've forgotten to ask you who we're staying with tonight."

"As a matter of fact, Nanny, you will be sleeping in a train on our way to Paris."

"*To Paris*!" Nanny exclaimed. "You never told me we were going there!"

"I have only just made up my mind, because I had so many invitations from my friends before I left school. I refused them because I did not know that Papa was going away. Now as he has gone North, I thought it was a good time for you and me to travel and we will be back home before he returns."

"Well, I certainly never thought that I'd be finding myself going to Paris, but it'll be an experience."

"It is a beautiful city, Nanny, and I am sure you will enjoy it very much."

"Where are we staying in Paris?" Nanny asked.

"You remember Cousin Violet? She is now Lady Walton?"

"I thinks I do remember her," replied Nanny. "But I thought she lived abroad – "

"She does, she lives in Paris, where she has been since her husband died. He was in the Diplomatic Service and became a British Ambassador."

"Her Ladyship must be pretty old by now," Nanny commented.

"Actually she is ill and bedridden, but I used to call to see her once a month when I was at school, because she liked to talk of the old days and what a success her parties always were."

She did not add that Lady Walton was now almost senile and had really no idea of what was going on around her.

She had visited her because she thought it was her duty and her father liked to have news of his cousin.

But Malvina had known the last time she went that Lady Walton had not the faintest idea who she was or why she had come.

However, she lived in a comfortable house in the *Faubourg St. Honoré*, not far from the British Embassy.

Malvina thought it would be quite easy for her and Nanny to stay there.

The train ride to Dover did not take too long.

The courier had arranged that Malvina should have a private cabin in the ferry that was to carry them to Calais.

They were fortunate to procure it as there were only two private cabins on board and there was usually a large demand for them.

Malvina hurried into her cabin, thinking it would be a mistake to be seen by any of the crowd on the ferry.

She certainly did not want to be recognised by any of her father's friends as they would undoubtedly question her as to where she was travelling to and why he was not accompanying her.

They reached Calais without any incidents on the way.

The train to Paris was waiting for them and it was a great relief to find there was one of the new sleeper salons attached to it.

The courier had arranged a First Class compartment for Malvina with one for Nanny next door.

"I'll tell the Steward, my Lady, exactly where I'll be and if you need me, he'll inform me at once."

"Thank you, thank you very much," said Malvina. "I am so delighted to have this comfortable compartment, when I was afraid I might have to sit up all night."

The courier smiled.

"All the latest trains to Paris have a sleeper these days, my Lady, and they are very much more comfortable, I'm told, than they were when they first started."

The train began to shunt slowly out of the station and Malvina could not resist running out into the corridor to watch them move away.

As she turned to go back into her compartment, a voice called out,

"Surely it is Malvina Silisley! I thought I caught a glimpse of you on the ferry."

She looked round in surprise and saw the Comte de Michlet – his sister had been one of her closest friends at the Finishing School in St. Cloud.

Because Deirdre's family owned a house in Paris as well as their château on the Loire, Malvina had spent a lot of time with them.

She had often lunched with them in Paris and had once been to stay in their beautiful château.

The Comte de Michlet was Deirdre's eldest brother and he had not concerned himself with the two schoolgirls.

Yet now Malvina realised his eyes were appraising her.

She looked very different with her hair done up and wearing clothes that were much smarter than those she had worn at school.

"Why are you going to Paris?" he asked her.

"My father has gone to Scotland and I thought it would be a good opportunity to go to see my cousin, Lady Walton, who has been ill for a long time."

"That is most kind of you," said the Comte. "But it seems to be a waste of a visit to Paris if that is all you are going to do."

Malvina smiled at him.

"I can think of other things, but it may be difficult. I have come away at a moment's notice and so no one is aware of my impending arrival."

"Well, I am aware of it now," the Comte remarked. "So let's sit down and you tell me what you want to see in Paris that would be different from what you saw when you were at the school."

Malvina led the way into her compartment.

She guessed that Nanny was already lying down as she had felt seasick when they were crossing the Channel.

"Now please tell me what you would like to do," the Comte persisted and he settled himself comfortably on the seat that could be turned into a bed.

"I think it is for you to tell me what is happening in Paris now," Malvina answered him. "We used to hear all sorts of stories when Deirdre and I were at school, but I am not sure whether they were the truth or part of someone's imagination."

"What sort of stories?"

Malvina gave a little laugh.

"I do not need to tell you that. I used to hear from Deirdre which lovely lady you were with at the time, and the other girls with brothers or cousins were also curious about the gay life of Paris."

The Comte chuckled.

"I must say I would never have thought my sister would talk about my *affaires!*"

"We used to hear just how the beautiful women you entertained in Paris made each party ever more outrageous and more expensive than the last."

"Expensive is the right word, and it is a good thing you cannot go to those parties. One in the family is quite enough."

"Unfortunately," Malvina told him, "I have not got a brother so I was unable to join in with any spicy tales."

She paused before she added,

"As a matter of fact I am rather interested in finding out what one particular young gentleman is doing at the moment."

"Why are you interested in him? As a suitor?"

Malvina shook her head.

"No, nothing like that. I have not even met him. But Papa is an old friend of his father, who, I understand, is rather worried about his son's extravagance and the way he is behaving."

"That can apply to a great number of gentlemen," the Comte reflected. "If you tell me who he is, them I will see if I know him."

"His father is the Marquis of Arramford," Malvina told him, "and the young gentleman is the Earl of Arram."

"Then, of course, I know him. Charles is one of the gentlemen one meets at every party to which you, my dear Malvina, would not want to be allowed to attend."

"Tell me more about the parties," pleaded Malvina. "I expect Deirdre knows about them."

"Well, at the last one I was at, which was about a week ago, the hostess was carried in by four footmen."

"Why was she carried?"

"She was sitting in what appeared to be a huge soup tureen, and when the lid was removed she sprang up out of it wearing very little, but looking exceedingly glamorous."

The Comte laughed before he added,

"The dish had a special name, but it is one I will not repeat to you, because it is not for your ears."

"And you found that dinner enjoyable?"

"It was certainly most unusual and highly amusing for those who were taking part in it."

"Was the Earl one of them?" asked Malvina.

"Very much so. In fact he was the host."

"And who was the hostess?"

"I suppose I should not be indiscreet, but I cannot think it matters as you do not live in Paris – "

"Oh, do tell me!" insisted Malvina coaxingly. "It is all so fascinating."

"Well, Charles was actually enjoying an *affaire-de-coeur* with a most fascinating young woman called Cora Pearl. It was of course she who was in the soup tureen and there is no doubt that she is very alluring."

Malvina was listening to the Comte, wide-eyed.

As if he enjoyed having someone to talk to, he went on,

"His last *affaire-de-coeur* had been, in my opinion, with an even more attractive woman."

"And who was that?"

"She is known as Blanche d'Antigny. She is one of the most famous Paris beauties and in the theatre where she appeared in many plays and all the audiences admired her beauty."

The way he spoke told Malvina without words that Blanche d'Antigny had appeared with very little on.

However, as she was interested in her because she had been attached to Charles Arram, she enquired,

"And what is she doing now?"

"She has a very nice house that someone must have paid for, and has become a star of the Palais-Royal. That she is an undoubted success, not only on the stage but off it, is shown by the brilliance of her diamonds."

"Diamonds! Surely she could not afford to acquire those herself."

The Comte looked at her and she realised that she had said something rather stupid.

"That was silly of me," she admitted. "Of course, as she is so attractive, they were given to her."

"She makes certain of it," the Comte added, "and a great number of young men have spent a fortune not only on her diamonds but on her clothes."

"You mean her clothes are also paid for by men?"

"In the second act of *Le Chateau à Toto* which has the most marvellous music by Offenbach, Blanche wore a dress costing sixteen thousand francs. In the third act she wore an amazing transparent peignoir costing six thousand francs and every woman in Paris was green with envy."

"I am not surprised," exclaimed Malvina.

"I did not see her in the show at the Palais-Royal," the Comte continued, "but I do understand that she was a huge success. I have heard now, however, that the young man you are interested in, Charles Arram, has left her."

"If she is so incredibly beautiful, why has he done so?" enquired Malvina.

The Comte shrugged his shoulders.

"I do think, Charles Arram, like most men, likes a change. But he will find his new interest very much more expensive than anything Blanche asked for in her charming house in the *Avenue de Friedland*."

Malvina felt her head was whirling with all that she was learning.

She somehow never imagined the *cocottes* of Paris had comfortable houses of their own.

She had underestimated the amount of money that was spent on them despite what the girls had said at school.

Now she could understand why the Marquis was so worried about his son, Charles, and why at home he was finding it hard to make both ends meet.

Of course, he really wanted a rich daughter-in-law and doubtless Charles had a large number of debts which were still unpaid.

Malvina sat talking with the Comte, who obviously enjoyed the sound of his own voice till it was nearly time for dinner.

"You must dine with me, Malvina, but as I intend to change my clothes and be more comfortable, I will come and fetch you in half-an-hour's time."

Malvina was uncertain whether this was something correct for her to do, but there was no one she could ask.

It seemed harmless enough to dine with the brother of one of her greatest friends on a train.

When the Comte had left, she told Nanny what she was doing.

Nanny took it calmly.

"You'd better change, Malvie," she now suggested. "I'll do you up, but I don't want to get out of bed because I still feels a bit sick from that nasty sea."

Malvina thought it had been fairly calm, but did not say so.

She changed into a light frock and Nanny buttoned it up at the back.

"I believe we are arriving early tomorrow, at about eight o'clock, so I will not be late, Nanny, but if you are asleep, I will not wake you."

"You wake me up if you can't undo yourself. I'm used to sleeping with one eye open, as you well know."

Malvina smiled.

She remembered when a child that if she gave just a whisper Nanny would come to her bed to see if anything was wrong.

She tidied her hair and she thought, without being conceited, that the new way Nanny was doing it was very attractive.

She waited for the Comte who had changed into a velvet smoking jacket.

His collar and tie were immaculate.

She thought as they walked along the corridor that people they passed looked at them with admiration.

The Comte had already booked a table for two at the furthest end of the dining car, where they would not be disturbed.

As soon as they sat down, he started to talk about the amusements of Paris.

Malvina listened to him attentively.

As dinner was served he began to pay her a number of compliments.

Then he remarked,

"As Deirdre is staying away with my parents in the country, I am sorry I cannot invite you to stay at our house rather than with your cousin, Lady Walton."

"It is very kind of you," Malvina said quickly, "but I must go to her as she always looks forward to my visits."

"If I may I will call on you whilst you are in Paris, and I am sure that there will be a party given by one of my mother's friends I can invite you to."

"It is certainly very good of you, but I will not be staying long. You have certainly made the journey much more interesting for me than I had expected."

"You have grown very lovely since you were at that school," sighed the Comte.

Malvina thanked him, but smiled to herself.

She realised that when she was just a schoolgirl, the Comte had not shown the least interest in her.

He had quite obviously been absorbed then in some fascinating beauty like Blanche d'Antigny.

Somewhat indiscreetly he told her the names of the two other *cocottes* who Charles Arram had been interested in for a short while.

"His affairs never last long," he confided lightly. "I personally find it hard to make a change, even though one is often tempted to do so."

While they were dining, he drank a great deal of champagne.

By the time that dinner was finished he became less cautious about what he was saying.

"If you ask me," he replied to one question Malvina asked him, "your father's friend, the Marquis, would be wise to make Charles go home. He is spending too much time and too much money on these temptresses who empty a man's pocket every time he looks at them!"

"So why do you find them so attractive?" Malvina asked innocently.

She was still somewhat vague about what happened when these bejewelled women looked with favour at a man like Charles or the Comte.

The Comte laughed at her question.

"I think the truth is a man feels that he is a clever fellow to possess anything so lovely. It is like owning the winning horse in the best race of the Season. You know all your contemporaries are regarding you with envy."

Then he gave what was almost a sigh, as he added,

"At the same time the moment comes when one can spend no more."

Malvina wanted to ask why a woman cost so much, but she thought it was a rather embarrassing question.

Finally she bade the Comte goodnight and thanked him for her dinner.

She thought she had learnt exactly what she wanted to know and should be very grateful to him.

Her bed had been made up by the Steward while she was at dinner.

Without waking up Nanny, she managed to slip out of her dress and climb into the small bed.

Despite the rumbling wheels beneath her and the fact that she felt excited by all that she had heard from the Comte, she slept peacefully.

*

She was woken by the Steward who then informed her that they would be coming into the *Gare du Nord* in an hour's time.

Nanny was already dressed and having recovered from her sea-sickness, she helped Malvina into her clothes.

"Did you have a nice dinner?" she asked.

"It was very interesting, Nanny. I learnt a lot about Paris that I had not known before."

"Well, that's nice for you. Now put on your hat. It'll not be long now before we're at the station."

Malvina did as she was told.

She then stepped out of her compartment to find the courier collecting their luggage.

The Comte appeared looking a little bleary-eyed.

"I will tell Deirdre you are in Paris," he said. "But I do not think she will be back from the country for a week or so."

"I don't think we shall be staying that long," she answered. "But give her my love, and thank you again for a most interesting dinner."

"I hope I did not shock you, Malvina."

"No, of course not," she replied.

"I thought as I climbed into bed last night that you were a bit young for listening to that sort of talk. But I do suppose you have to grow up some time."

"I have grown up, what you have told me was very helpful."

He took off his hat just as his valet appeared with a porter carrying his luggage.

"I have some engagements for the next two or three nights, but we might dine together later on in the week."

"That would be lovely, but I think perhaps I ought to have a chaperone."

She saw by the expression in the Comte's eyes that this was something he had not intended.

Then he added hurriedly,

"Goodbye and enjoy yourself in Paris."

"I am sure I will," Malvina answered doubtfully.

He walked away from her and the courier appeared a few moments later with their luggage.

They hired a carriage and drove to Lady Walton's house in the *Faubourg St. Honoré*.

When they had arrived at their destination, Malvina explained to the servants that she and Nanny had come to stay with them for a few nights.

She had been there before and they welcomed her most sincerely.

She was taken up to the best bedroom after the one occupied by Cousin Violet.

One of the nurses attending Lady Walton came to see Malvina, as she was taking off her travelling clothes.

"I am afraid that her Ladyship is not at all well," the nurse informed her.

"I am so sorry," answered Malvina.

"She's in a coma most of the time," the nurse went on, "but she's in no pain and there's nothing the doctors can do for her."

Malvina went with the nurse in to see her father's cousin.

There was no doubt that Lady Walton had changed a great deal over the years Malvina had known her. She had been good-looking and distinguished. Now she seemed small and emaciated and her face was very lined.

Her hair was dead white and with her eyes closed she looked very different from how Malvina remembered her when she had visited Silstone Court.

When she returned to her own bedroom, she put on one of her prettiest day dresses with a little short coat to wear over it.

She had a hat to go with it and she thought when she glanced at herself in the mirror that she looked quite smart, but at the same time not in the least flashy.

She went into Nanny's room which was near her own.

"I am just going across to the Embassy, Nanny, and I will not be long and there is no need for you to come with me."

"Well, that's a good thing, I'm a bit tired as I didn't sleep well last night."

"Oh, I am sorry. Have you got a headache?"

"Not a bad one, and I'll be all right in an hour or so. Just you run along, Malvie, and I expect you'll be back for luncheon."

"Of course I will, unless they ask me to stay at the Embassy. Don't wait for me, but I am sure I will be back."

She ran downstairs and told the butler that she was going to visit the Embassy and, as it was only a short walk away, there was no need for her to take a conveyance.

He bowed politely and opened the door for her.

When she heard the front door close behind her, she started to hurry.

She walked straight down the *Faubourg St. Honoré* and passed the British Embassy without stopping.

Then she hailed a passing fiacre and as she climbed into it, she instructed the driver,

"Take me to number 11 *Avenue de Friedland.*"

He nodded his reply.

As they drove off Malvina knew that she was doing what her father and every relation she had would consider outrageous and disgraceful.

Yet it was a scheme that she had plotted carefully in her own mind.

It was, she knew, the only way she could find out the whole truth – the only way she could make sure that what she suspected about the Earl of Arram was so very different from the way her father regarded him.

Most of all she had no intention of marrying a man who would spend her money as he had spent his father's.

It did not take long for the fiacre to carry Malvina across the *Place de la Concorde.*

It was always a joy and a delight to see it, except that she could not help remembering that the guillotine had stood in one corner.

Louis XVI had climbed the steps onto the scaffold, but this morning all the fountains were playing and the sun was shining brightly.

However Malvina was thinking only of the exciting adventure to which she had dedicated herself.

It was an adventure which seemed at the moment totally unreal and yet she had a feeling within herself that it would be the solution to her problem.

Perhaps to all the problems that may lie ahead in the future.

It gave her a start when the horse pulling the fiacre stopped outside an impressive house.

Just for a moment Malvina felt that what she was asking was too much – and perhaps she should drive on.

Then she told herself firmly that one thing she must not be is a coward.

The man driving the fiacre came down from his box and opened the door for her.

She asked him to wait for her and he agreed.

She walked up to the door in front of her and as it had a polished silver knocker, she rapped it.

There was a pause before the door was opened by a liveried footman.

He was just as smart as the footmen they employed at home and this was somewhat of a surprise for Malvina.

"I am Lady Malvina Silisley," she said to him in her excellent French. "Would it be possible for me to see Madame d'Antigny? I have just arrived from England and I have a special message that I think she will be interested to hear."

"I will go and ask Madame if she will see you," the footman replied.

He led the way through a large hall which was hung with tapestries and decorated with exotic plants.

There were many flowers in baskets and bouquets that had obviously recently been delivered at the house.

The footman then led Malvina to a salon which was certainly impressive. Chandeliers hung from the ceiling, tapestries lent a mystery to the walls and the curtains were of blue velvet.

It was all so different from what Malvina had been expecting.

She thought too it was in surprisingly good taste for a *cocotte*.

The ornate clock resting on the mantelpiece was in the form of a statuette of Peter the Great.

It reminded Malvina that later last night, when the Comte had drunk a great deal, he had spoken of Blanche d'Antigny again.

He described how she had attracted the attention of a Russian Prince, who was so enamoured with her that he was determined to set her up in a Palace in St. Petersburg.

This was no doubt his plan to remove her from his rivals and, according to the Comte, Blanche had the French Nobles fighting over her 'like dogs'.

"During that spring," the Comte confided, "Blanche consistently refused the Prince's offer. When the summer came, however, and many people had by then left Paris for the country, she did permit him to take her to Wiesbaden. There she created a sensation and gambled wildly."

He paused for a moment and then chuckled,

"So wildly in fact that when the Season finished the Prince was most relieved when he was able to take her to

St. Petersburg. She then spent four years in Russia and the constant applause and admiration went to her head."

Lowering his voice, the Comte had carried on,

"In spite of strict protocol, she decided to attend the traditional Gala Performance that ended the Winter Season at the Opera. She was so determined to wear a gown that would outshine both the actresses and the audience."

This Malvina could understand.

"It must have been a very difficult thing to do," she commented.

"No," the Comte replied, "she found exactly what she wanted – the dress was superb as it had been ordered by the Czarina. The couturier protested that Blanche could not have it, but she would not listen. She thrust a bundle of notes into his hand and hurried out of the shop with the gown in her arms."

"What happened?" Malvina asked breathlessly.

The Comte had thrown up his hands as he said,

"The next day she was expelled from Russia!"

Malvina had found the story enthralling.

Now as she looked at the little statue of Peter the Great, she wondered if Blanche had wept on her way here.

Or had she just taken it as another knock of fate on the road to reach the top?

Even as Malvina asked herself this question, the door opened.

She expected it to be the footman to tell her if his Mistress would see her.

The man opened the door wide.

"If you will now please follow me, mademoiselle," he said, "I will take you upstairs."

CHAPTER THREE

The footman led Malvina up a long staircase and by some very attractive pictures.

Then he opened a door and announced in an almost stentorian voice,

"Lady Malvina Silisley, madame."

Malvina walked in.

At first glance it was the most glamorous bedroom she had ever seen.

A big four-poster bed was hung with turquoise satin and under an enormous baldaquin with blue silk and lace curtains it looked like a throne half hidden by clouds.

Sitting against a pile of richly lace-edged pillows was a very lovely woman.

Malvina had expected, from all she had heard about Blanche d'Antigny, that she would be extremely attractive.

But she had not expected a milk-white complexion on a French woman.

Her cheeks were faintly tinted with rose pink and her eyes seemed almost childish.

At the same time they were sparkling like stars.

As she held out a hand of slender beautiful fingers, Malvina could well understand why she was such a huge success with men.

Blanche d'Antigny was regarding her curiously.

Malvina knew it was because she was puzzled as to why she had called to see her.

She shook hands and then sat down on a chair that was arranged beside the bed.

"You must please forgive me, madame," she began in French, "for calling on you without an introduction but I desperately need your help."

"My help!" exclaimed Blanche. "Why?"

Malvina sat a little more comfortably on the chair.

"It is rather embarrassing to explain and I hope you will not be offended – "

Blanche laughed.

"I am seldom offended by anything, except when people are rude and I am hoping you will not be."

"No, of course not, madame, but I heard about you from the brother of a friend of mine, and I felt you were the one person who could help me solve an extremely difficult problem to which I can at present find no solution."

Blanche lay back against her lace pillows.

"Please tell me all about it."

A little shyly, Malvina started to tell her story,

"I have come to visit Paris without anyone at home knowing where I am."

"Surely not *alone*!"

"Oh no, of course not, madame, I have brought my old Nanny along with me and I am staying with an elderly relation, who is seriously ill and lives in the *Faubourg St. Honoré*."

Malvina stopped speaking and there was a silence and then Blanche remarked,

"I am wondering how I can be concerned in your problems."

"I think," Malvina said hesitantly, "that you – know the Earl of Arram very well."

Blanche's beautiful eyes widened.

"Of course, I do. Charles has been a friend of mine for several years."

"That is what I was told by the Comte de Michlet."

She saw by the expression in Blanche's eyes that she knew who the Comte was, as she continued,

"When I came home, having been at the Convent School in St. Cloud, I found out that my own father and the Marquis of Arramford had decided between themselves that I should marry the Earl. As I have not seen him since I was a small child, I very much resent being forced into an arranged marriage with someone I do not know."

Blanche gave a little laugh.

"I can understand your feelings, mademoiselle, but in France our aristocrats always have arranged marriages, as do Royalty. So I suppose your father and the Marquis considered that they were in the same category."

"I think that any arranged marriage is horrifying!"

"I agree with you," said Blanche, "but as you are so young, I doubt if they will listen to your protest."

"That is what I feel myself, madame, and is why I have come to see you."

Again Blanche looked surprised.

"I still cannot quite see what I can do about it," she murmured.

"What I want, if it is possible," said Malvina, "is to see Charles Arram socially without his realising who I am and thus being on his best behaviour. If he does do things that would shock or upset my father, I shall not be aware of them if he knows who I am."

She paused for a moment and realised that Blanche was listening intently.

"I have heard stories that he lives a most frivolous and extravagant life in Paris. What I am begging you to do, madame, is to help me by letting me see him when he has no idea he is being watched and perhaps criticised."

As Malvina finished speaking, Blanche threw her head back and let out a loud laugh.

"This is something I have never been asked before, and I think it most amusing. Also I think it is very brave of you to come here and attempt anything so unusual."

"I feel it is the only way that I might be able to save myself – "

"Of course it is, my dear, and that shows you are very intelligent."

"It is difficult to know exactly how you can help me, madame, but I have brought a wig with me so that I can disguise myself and so that if I saw him with others, he need not even know I am English."

Now there was a pleading note in her voice and she felt instinctively that Blanche d'Antigny was hesitating to help her as she was requesting.

There was a short silence.

"I suppose what you are thinking could be possible, mademoiselle. In fact it might even happen tonight."

"*Tonight*!" cried Malvina.

"I am giving a dinner party, as it so happens, and I have special reasons for doing so – "

She regarded Malvina calculatingly as if she was wondering whether she could trust her with the truth.

Then she continued,

"I expect the Comte de Michlet, whom I only know slightly but who undoubtedly knows a great deal about me, has told you that my affair with Charles has finished."

Malvina nodded.

"Yes, he did mention it."

"I suppose if one is notorious," admitted Blanche, "or famous is the word I would prefer, it is what one must expect."

"From what the Comte told me, madame, you are indeed famous and everyone admires you tremendously."

Blanche smiled.

"That is what I like to think. Although Charles has left me, I am very fortunate in having a fascinating friend to look after me – the Prince de Trémere."

"He is French?" asked Malvina.

"Yes, he is, and to be honest with you it is rather a relief after coping with the vagaries and peculiarities of an Englishman!"

Malvina laughed.

"I am sure Charles Arram, although I do not know him, does not think himself peculiar."

"No, of course not," agreed Blanche. "But he is so fond of his own importance and actually believes that any woman he patronises is very lucky."

Now there was a sharp note in her voice and it told Malvina without words that she was annoyed with the Earl.

She thought that this might help her cause and she added quickly,

"You do see, it is so very frightening to be told you have to marry someone of whom you know nothing except that he pursues beautiful women and spends a great deal of money he cannot afford."

"I rather thought that was the case. He told me that when he went home he had a furious row with his father. And what do fathers and sons row about if not *money?*"

She said the last few words in a manner that made Malvina laugh.

"And you think I can meet the Earl with you?" she asked.

"I am giving a dinner party tonight with my friend the Prince and, because I wanted to show Charles that I do not miss him in any way, I have invited him and his new friend, Cora Pearl, of whom I expect you have heard."

"The Comte did mention her."

"She is English and a great success in Paris, and has a special affection for gentlemen with a title. I am quite certain that if Charles was not an Earl, she would not even have looked at him."

Again there was a sharp and rather spiteful note in Blanche's voice.

Malvina said quickly,

"Oh, please, please let me come to your party. It would be just so wonderful for me to have such an unusual experience and to see Charles Arram in his element."

For a moment Blanche did not reply.

But the way she was looking at her told Malvina she was considering if she could be disguised sufficiently for her other guests not to be curious about her.

Malvina sent up a little prayer that Blanche would agree to do what she so wanted.

Finally, after what seemed to Malvina a long time Blanche d'Antigny, said,

"You say you have a wig that will prevent you from looking so English, and, of course, my maid can make up your face. You could not attend my party as you look now without everyone being extremely curious about you."

"I will do whatever you tell me, madame, and it is very kind and wonderful of you even to consider it."

"Then what I think that we must now do," Blanche suggested, "is to arrange for you to come here early in the evening when it is time for us to dress. But not too early as my friend will be with me."

She thought for a moment.

"My hairdresser will put on your wig, and I will, if you are agreeable, let you borrow one of my gowns."

Malvina clapped her hands together.

"Can I really do that? Oh, *how* kind of you! I was wondering if I should go out and buy the sort of dress I should wear. But I am not certain I would choose the right fashion."

"If we have to keep up this pretence longer than tonight, you will go to my couturier, who is naturally the most famous in Paris. But I am afraid you might find him rather expensive."

"I do not have to worry about money, madame. My father is a very rich man, and I am convinced that is the real reason that Charles Arram's father, the Marquis, wants me as his daughter-in-law."

Blanche threw her hands in the air in a very French gesture.

"Now, of course, I understand," she cried. "Charles certainly needs a great deal more money to spend on Cora Pearl, who is so famed for making a man bankrupt quicker than any other woman in the whole of France!"

Malvina realised again that there was a harsh tone in Blanche's voice.

She noticed that, despite the fact that she now had the Prince in tow, Blanche was still feeling very angry that Charles Arram had left her.

Aloud she proposed,

"If I can come to you, madame, at exactly the hour

you tell me, I can only thank you from the bottom of my heart for being so kind and so understanding."

"Of course I appreciate that a very pretty girl – no a beautiful girl – like you, who is also English, wants to marry a man who loves her for herself and someone who is likely to be faithful."

She gave a little sigh before she added,

"Englishmen on the whole are much more faithful than men of other nations in Europe. But Charles has said over and over again he has no wish to be married."

"That is just what I thought," nodded Malvina, "and I am therefore determined, if it is humanly possible, *not* to be married for my money."

"With your good looks it would be an unforgivable insult. Now, *ma chère*, we have everything fixed. You are to come here at precisely six o'clock when my hairdresser will be waiting for you."

"Oh, thank you, thank you so much, madame, I was very nervous at coming to see you, but you have been so kind and are doing for me what I am sure no other woman would do."

Blanche smiled and reached across the bed to ring a gold bell on the table beside her.

The door was opened immediately by her maid.

"Show her Ladyship downstairs," ordered Blanche. "She will be returning here this evening when Félix will do her hair and you will make her up.

"She will be wearing one of my gowns, one which I have not worn for a long time so that no one will remember it. And you will have to make her grace my party as one of my most beautiful guests."

The maid grinned.

"That will be easy, madame. I will have everything ready."

"Thank you again, thank you very much," enthused Malvina.

She rose from the chair where she had been sitting and then hesitated.

"I want to give you something for being so kind to me, but as you have the most beautiful flowers everywhere, I cannot think what it should be."

Blanche smiled.

"Let us leave it and we will talk about it later when your mission to Paris is over and you have achieved what you came here for."

Malvina smiled at her.

Then she went towards the door and as she reached it, she turned and looked back.

She thought that no woman could be lovelier than Blanche looked in her glamorous blue four-poster bed.

Malvina realised now that a white bearskin served as a rug and on a consol table stood a figure of Christ.

The maid closed the door of the bedroom.

Next to it was another door which Malvina realised was Blanche's bathroom where the bath was made of the finest marble.

It suddenly made her recall that the Comte, droning on towards the end of dinner, had told her,

"Blanche has two hundred bottles of Montebello poured into her bath when she is feeling particularly tired!"

The maid took her downstairs.

The large pile of flowers in the hall had increased considerably since she had been upstairs.

She glanced at them considering that they were not only beautiful but very expensive.

Now there now were two footmen in smart livery in the hall.

The one who had escorted her upstairs opened the door for her. He took her down the steps and helped her into the fiacre which was still waiting for her.

He bowed politely as she thanked him and drove away.

They went back the way they had come, but by now Malvina was too intent on her thoughts to enjoy the beauty of Paris.

Even now she could scarcely believe that she had achieved what she had set out to do.

What had seemed an almost impossible plan to see Charles Arram when he was off guard had now been made possible – thanks to Blanche d'Antigny.

Equally she felt a strange mixture of fear at what she had undertaken and a degree of triumph that she had so far been successful.

When she returned to Lady Walton's house, no one appeared to have missed her.

Nanny merely asked if she had found her friends.

"Yes, I found them, Nanny, and I am going to dine with them this evening."

"Oh, that'll be nice, I was just thinking it must be rather dull for you to stay in Paris and not have a chance of enjoying the parties that I've always been told are so unlike those in England."

Malvina discreetly smiled that Nanny would think very differently if she only knew whose party she would be attending that very evening!

She had a feeling she herself would find it strange.

At the same time rather frightening, as she did not know how she should behave at Blanche's dinner party.

She went upstairs to her bedroom and opened her hat-box, which had not been unpacked since she arrived.

She took out the hats she had brought with her and then she came to the wig that had belonged to her aunt.

It was certainly made of the very best hair and she thought it must have been exceedingly expensive.

Certainly her aunt had looked lovely in it even when she was very old.

Malvina found a small box in a cupboard in which she concealed the wig as she knew it would be a mistake for Nanny to ask questions as to why she had it with her and where she was taking it.

The afternoon would have passed slowly if she had not found the newspapers that had been brought into the house.

They were there clearly not for its owner, but for the nurses who looked after her.

There was reference in their Social columns to what was taking place in Paris at present.

One newspaper that was well known to be slightly scandalous, reported more of the gay life of Paris than the more respectable ones.

Malvina discovered that Prince Napoleon had been 'the protector', if that was the right word, of Cora Pearl.

The newspaper wrote that as the Prince received a million francs a year from the Civil List, he could afford to be generous.

He had therefore established Cora Pearl in 101 *Rue de Chaillot*, which was a veritable Palace and came to be known as *Les Petites Tuileries*.

In fact it was widely whispered around that he gave

her twelve thousand francs every month on the strength of which she regularly spent more than double.

The newspaper went on to say that she bathed in a rose marble bathroom with her initials inlaid in gold on the bottom of the bath.

As she bathed she could gaze at her portrait which smiled down on her from the bathroom wall.

But dissatisfied, the paper continued, with a single house, Cora had allowed the Prince Napoleon to buy her a second one in 6 *Rue des Bassins*.

Having read all this Malvina realised the newspaper she was reading was several months old and they had all been piled into a cupboard in the sitting room.

Because she was interested to see if more had been written about Cora Pearl, she looked at the more up-to-date editions.

She found one which said that she had appeared as Eve at a fancy-dress ball – her form and figure were not concealed by anything more than was worn by the original apple-eater!

Another newspaper published a year ago reported that Cora Pearl had made her appearance half naked on a stage.

She had sung with a marked Anglo-Saxon accent some couplets which began, '*I know love –* '

That evening the entire Jockey Club had graced the theatre and all the names that are blazoned in the Golden Book of the French Nobility were present, complete with white gloves and ivory lorgnettes.

The Duc de Gramont-Caderousse had summed her up in a phrase that the French found very amusing,

'*If the Frères Provencaux served omelettes studded with diamonds, Cora would go and dine with them every evening*'.

There was another story in a newspaper that when she had appeared at the *Bouffes Theatre*, she dropped two diamonds onto the stage and left them for her dresser to retrieve.

They were each worth four thousand francs, which was twice the dresser's annual wage.

The writer of the article remarked cynically that if the tale was true, Cora Pearl could surely spare the jewels and added,

'*She looked like a jeweller's window with daylight lighting.*'

Another newspaper described how she had created a sensation with her appearance at the theatre.

A Comte had offered fifty thousand francs for the boots she wore on the stage. This was because the buttons on her boots were of the largest diamonds of the purest type.

However the newspaper was not so complimentary about her theatrical talent, but needless to say she ignored any criticism.

It was obvious that few women led so resplendent a career as a *courtesan*.

There were pictures of her visit to the Universal Exhibition, while the Prince waited for her in his private room, which was furnished in Turkish style.

Another reported that she travelled to Monte Carlo where she lost a large amount of money – undoubtedly not hers.

In the same year it was widely reported that Cora had fought a duel in the Bois de Boulogne with another of the *courtesans*, Marthe de Vere.

It was all over a particularly handsome Serbian or Armenian Prince and it was recounted that both the women used their riding-whips freely and did considerable damage to each other's faces.

They did not reappear in public for a week during which time the Prince vanished.

Malvina put down the newspapers and gave a sigh.

If this was the sort of person Charles Arram wanted to be with, he was *not* likely to be amused by her.

In another newspaper she found the story she had already heard of how Cora gave a supper party, where she had many white orchids strewn over the floor that Prince Napoleon had sent her in a large van.

She then danced a hornpipe on them, dressed as a sailor, followed by the can-can.

The journalist who had reported this remembered a similar occasion when the Prince had sent her a basket of flowers.

She had thrown them on the carpet and trampled on them, baying, 'I am tired of Princely admirers'.

This had all happened quite recently and it made Malvina think that was why she had left her Prince for the moment and apparently had fallen straight into the arms of Charles Arram.

Malvina was quite certain that he could not afford her under any circumstances and she appreciated now, if he had kept sending to his father for more and more money, how worried the Marquis must be.

She only had time to look through a few more of the newspapers and then as it was getting late, she put them back into the cupboard.

She wondered vaguely why they had been kept in the first place – perhaps the nurses found it amusing to read of the peculiar goings-on in other parts of Paris.

However, it all seemed very exciting to Malvina.

She could hardly wait for the hands of the clock to move steadily towards the time when she would go again to Blanche d'Antigny's house.

At five o'clock she went up the stairs to change her gown, tidy herself and collect her wig.

As she did so she reflected on how angry her father would be if he knew she was associating with the famous *courtesans* of Paris.

The nuns at the Convent School would raise their hands in sheer horror.

'It may be wrong, but I must know something about this man they want me to marry,' Malvina assured herself.

At the same time she knew, if she did what would be expected of an English Noblewoman, she would send a polite note to Blanche saying that she had now changed her mind.

But that, she told herself, would be a very cowardly thing to do.

After all, she had come to Paris determined to find out what Charles was doing.

Admittedly she had heard a bit about the *courtesans* when she was at the school, but not the sort of information she had just read in the newspapers.

The nuns had been very strict about what the girls read and only the dullest newspapers were allowed in the schoolroom.

What had been kept surprisingly in the cupboard of Lady Walton's sitting room were newspapers that she had never even heard of, let alone seen, when at school.

It seemed quite extraordinary that men like Prince Napoleon and the other members of the aristocracy should be so interested in the *cocottes* of Paris – even though they had an originality which could not be found in any other City.

Yet so much money had been spent on them and so much thrown away.

But whether the French liked it or not, the *cocottes* were part of their history.

Perhaps the whole scenario was all very shocking and something she should ignore.

But Malvina felt, having set her hand to the plough, she could not turn back.

At a quarter-to-six she went downstairs dressed in an evening gown over which she was wearing a satin cape.

Nanny was in the sitting room and called out,

"Oh, are you dressed, Malvie? If I had known, I'd have come up and helped you."

"I have managed fine. I hope you will be all right, Nanny, and not be too lonely here tonight."

"No, of course not. As you're going out, I'll have dinner with the nurses and cheer them up. They were only saying today how bored they are at never seeing a different face from one week's end to the next."

Malvina thought for a moment.

"If we stay here long enough, Nanny, perhaps we can look after Cousin Violet ourselves one night and send the nurses out to a theatre."

"That be a very kind thought of yours, Malvie, and that's the sort of thing your mother would have said. Yes, of course, we'll do it. In fact I could do it alone, if you had a nice invitation from your friends."

She had risen to her feet as she was speaking.

Now she inspected Malvina to see if she was tidy and that nothing was amiss.

"You look real pretty tonight," she said, "and that's the truth. It seems to me you should be going out to dinner with a young gentleman. So I hopes there's plenty of them to admire you when you arrives at your friends' house."

"I expect there will be plenty of people there and I hope I shall not be too late back."

"Well, do wake me up if I've gone to sleep, and I'll undo your gown."

Malvina kissed her.

"You are very kind, Nanny, and I love having you with me here in Paris."

Nanny smiled.

"Now get along with you," she urged, "and have a really good evening. I hopes perhaps you'll be dancing."

"I don't know about dancing – "

The butler hailed a fiacre for her.

She was sensible enough to have written down the address on a piece of paper, so that she did not have to say it aloud.

She handed the paper to the driver herself, so that there was no chance of the butler having a look at it.

Then he closed the door and she drove off.

She was pondering that whatever happened tonight it would be an adventure and something no other girl of her acquaintance would ever do.

'It will be something to write about in my memoirs if I ever get round to writing them,' she thought. 'Perhaps it will be something to make my husband, if I marry, laugh because it will be all so unexpected.'

She had the idea that if her husband did turn out to be Charles Arram, he would think very differently.

What she was really doing was spying on him and that was something no man expected when he thought he was completely safe well away from his family in a strange country.

But Malvina refused to feel sorry for him.

After all, if he was wasting money on someone like Cora Pearl, it was very wrong of him to do so.

He was well aware that his father was desperately in need of money for the house and the family estate.

And to throw away thousands of francs on a woman who was virtually covered with diamonds already was just extremely wrong.

'I suppose he thinks no one in England will know and that is why he stays over here in Paris,' she mused.

She wondered if she would be brave enough to tell him to go home and behave himself.

Then she laughed at the idea.

Equally the last man in the world she would want to marry was one who was constantly moving from *cocotte* to *cocotte* enjoying himself at the expense of his own family.

'I am certain it is something that Papa would never have done at any age,' she reflected.

Then she recalled that when her father was young and comparatively poor, he had visited Paris.

And he had wanted the enjoyment which apparently all men find so desirable.

'Just what have these women got that we have not?' asked Malvina – as many women had asked before her and many more would ask into the future.

Then she told herself that perhaps this was another secret she would learn tonight.

Even with what she had read about and what she had heard before she came to Paris, she was still very vague as to why the *cocottes* were so successful.

Why were they spoken of with bated breath?

Cora Pearl, she learnt from the newspapers, was the daughter of a Plymouth music teacher.

It seemed just so extraordinary that she should have become the sensation of the most glamorous and in many ways the most critical City in the whole of Europe.

Malvina was to learn later that Blanche d'Antigny was the eldest of three children of a carpenter, who lived in Martizay, a little town near Bourges in the Indre.

When Blanche, who was baptised Marie-Ernestine, was seven, her father had left his wife, running off with a local girl to Paris.

A year had passed before his wife set off in search of him, leaving the three children with their aunt.

Marie-Ernestine, with her lovely dark green eyes, champagne-coloured hair and a distinct white complexion, enjoyed an outdoor life.

She rode horses and wandered in the fields.

When her mother summoned her to Paris in 1850, she hid herself in an attic in despair as she could not bear the thought of leaving the countryside.

Malvina did not know this story at the moment.

She had no idea that Blanche, who was now being so kind to her, loved the country as much as she did.

She could only think of her as looking so beautiful – almost like a Goddess in her gigantic blue bed.

She found it difficult to believe that Charles Arram could find Cora Pearl more attractive than Blanche.

Of one thing she was quite convinced.

If Charles could leave anyone so lovely, he was not likely to be interested in an ordinary English girl.

Except for *one* reason – that she had money!

The fiacre drew up outside Blanche's door.

The same footman who had opened it earlier in the morning smiled at Malvina when she arrived.

"I'll take you to Madame's maid, mademoiselle," he said. "She is waiting for you upstairs."

"Thank you. That is very kind of you."

Carrying her wig carefully, she climbed the stairs.

The footman turned off just before they could reach Blanche's bedroom.

They went along a passage, then he knocked on the door at the end of it.

A voice called out,

"*Entrez!*"

The footman opened the door.

Blanche's maid, whom she had seen that morning, was standing by the dressing table.

And on it was arranged a variety of cosmetics.

Lying on the bed, a single one without any canopy, there was a gown.

At first glance Malvina realised that it was a very spectacular one.

"*Bonjour*, mademoiselle," the maid called out. "I have everything ready for you, but first we are expecting Monsieur Félix who you must know is the most famous hairdresser in the whole of Paris. He dresses the hair of the aristocratic ladies and every beautiful woman who wants to shine."

"I am so thrilled to have him do my hair," Malvina replied.

"He is expensive," the maid added meaningfully.

"I have brought a lot of money with me, and you must tell me what to give him."

The maid looked relieved and it seemed to Malvina strange that she should suspect that she might have her hair arranged without paying for it.

She now took off the cape she was wearing and sat down at the dressing table.

She had only just done so when the same footman opened the door again.

Monsieur Félix entered.

He was exactly as Malvina thought he would be.

He was rather thin but striking in a peculiar manner and obviously well aware of his own importance.

When she rose, shook his hand and thanked him for coming to do her hair, he nodded his approval.

He inspected her almost as if she was some queer creature come from outer space rather than a normal young woman.

"Now, mademoiselle," he began, "my instructions are to make you look completely different from how you look now."

"I am aware of that and I am sure, monsieur, you do understand that as well I must not look different from the other ladies present at the party tonight."

"You will look fully different," he replied, "for the simple reason, mademoiselle, that you are very much more beautiful than the majority of them."

He said this as if it was a simple fact rather than a compliment.

Malvina laughed.

"I only hope you are right, but please, monsieur, do what you can. And here is my wig."

Monsieur Félix inspected the wig as if he was quite certain it would not meet with his approval.

However, because it was such an expensive one and made of the very best hair, he did not make any comment.

By the time he had arranged it on Malvina's head, he

had completely altered the way it had been made for her aunt.

She had to admit that she did not look like herself.

In fact it seemed like an entirely unknown face that looked back at her from the mirror.

The maid, who had left the room, came back to say Madame Blanche was now alone and ready for Monsieur Félix when he was free.

He merely nodded to show that he understood.

But Malvina wondered who Blanche d'Antigny had been entertaining in her bedroom so early in the evening.

It all seemed to her so very strange and intriguing.

Then she told herself that everything would seem strange in this house where she had no right to be anyway.

Monsieur Félix left her, apparently content with the money she gave him.

The maid then started to make up her face, taking a great deal of trouble in doing so.

When finally she had finished, Malvina could hardly believe that she was indeed herself.

She was quite certain if her father came to the party he would not recognise her, neither would her friends from school.

Her eyes were enormous, seeming almost to fill her face.

Her skin was dazzlingly white with just a touch of colour on her cheeks.

Her lips were bright red as she had never seen them before.

As she looked at herself in the mirror the maid said,

"Madame thought that you might not have brought any jewellery with you. She has therefore loaned you a diamond necklace and some earrings which she said you would be expected to wear as her friend."

"That is most kind of her. Maybe I should put on the dress first to see if it fits me."

"I think you are the same size, mademoiselle, but, of course, I can pin you together if there is no other way the gown will fit."

The gown itself seemed fantastic to Malvina.

It was very beautiful, deep pink in colour and made of the very finest lace.

It was so *décolletée* at the front that she blushed as she looked at herself in the mirror.

It revealed her figure in a way as it had never been revealed before.

In fact Malvina had no idea at all that she had such beautifully shaped breasts, such a tiny waist or such narrow hips.

The lace clung to her skin and when she moved, it seemed as if the lace was a natural part of her.

It was beautifully embroidered round the neck and at the bottom with diamante and it glittered first in the light coming through the window, then later in the evening from the candles downstairs.

By this time Malvina was wearing a really lovely diamond necklace that glittered too.

She had diamonds round her wrist and in her ears.

She might have stepped straight off a stage rather than being about to walk into an ordinary reception room.

"I cannot believe *this* is me," she exclaimed to the maid.

"Madame will be very pleased when she sees you, and you will have the other ladies downstairs grinding their teeth with jealousy!"

"I don't want them to do that."

The maid laughed.

"Of course you do. It is wonderful the difference Monsieur Félix and Madame have made to you."

"That is certainly true," agreed Malvina. "I only hope I will not do anything wrong that will annoy her."

"Oh, she'll be all right as long as you don't take her new Prince away from her," the maid added in a familiar tone. "It were a bit of a shock when the last gentleman she fancied went off with that Cora Pearl.

"There's not many women has a good word for that one and the way that she goes on. But she has the Princes buzzing round her like bees round a honey pot and there's nothing anyone can do about it."

"Well, it is certain that I have no wish to take any man away from anyone," replied Malvina sincerely.

"If you sticks to that idea you'll be all right," the maid commented. "But to tell the truth I think it unlikely!"

Malvina laughed but equally she felt a little uneasy.

She had come to Paris to see what Charles Arram was doing and that was what she would find out tonight.

She had no wish to attract attention to herself or to take any woman's Prince away – that would undoubtedly lead to a great deal of trouble and acrimony.

'I must be very careful,' she told herself.

Then she walked down the stairs to where she had been instructed to meet Blanche d'Antigny in the reception room of her opulent house.

CHAPTER FOUR

A footman opened the door and Malvina walked in to a room she had seen on her earlier visit.

It was exceedingly attractive and very large and it seemed to be filled with flowers.

At first she thought there was no one else there.

Then Blanche rose from the sofa on which she had been sitting with a gentleman.

She was exquisitely if somewhat over-dressed in a gown that could easily have graced the finale of a theatrical performance.

Oh, here you are, *ma chèrie*," she said to Malvina. "I was just telling the Prince that my friend *Celeste Doré* was an extra guest tonight and I want you to meet him."

The way she emphasised the name told her that this was the name Blanche had given her for the evening.

She had been thinking as she came downstairs that they had not discussed what her *nom-de-plume* would be as she certainly could not join the party under her own name.

The man who rose from the sofa was good-looking but, Malvina thought, on the wrong side of forty.

Blanche said in her beguiling voice,

"Please allow me to introduce you, Garton dear, to my new friend Celeste, and I am sure you will think she is very pretty."

Prince Garton de Trémere now bowed politely over Malvina's hand.

Then he murmured as any Frenchman would do,

"I think that beautiful is the right description, *ma chère*."

"I bow," she sighed, "to your superior judgement, and of course, as I have told you before, *mon brave*, you are always right."

The Prince smiled at her.

Malvina watched the exchange of glances between the two.

She was sure that the Prince was in fact very much in love with Blanche d'Antigny.

It was not surprising, she thought, as no one could have looked lovelier or more entrancing than Blanche.

With diamonds glittering in her hair and round her neck she looked like a Goddess.

Her thin arms seemed literally to be weighed down with jewelled bracelets.

"I forgot to tell you," Blanche addressed Malvina, "that it is Cora Pearl's birthday tonight. That is why I am giving this special party for her."

She bent to pick up a parcel from one of the chairs.

"As we shall all be giving her a present later on, I thought you would like to give her this."

She handed Malvina a parcel wrapped in coloured paper and tied with bows of ribbon.

"What is inside?" Malvina asked, by now intrigued.

"You will see when she opens it, and it will be a surprise for you as well as for Cora."

As she finished speaking the door opened again and a footman announced the next guest.

After that they came in quick succession.

The women were extremely attractive and dressed

in the same way as Blanche was and they wore an immense amount of jewellery.

Of course, their faces were painted and their eyes mascaraed like Malvina's.

The gentlemen were all in evening dress and most of them boasted a title.

The footmen were handing round endless glasses of champagne.

Malvina watched Blanche receiving her guests and she thought as the room filled up that she was unlikely ever to be in a more fantastic or bejewelled party than this one.

The room seemed to be almost full when a footman announced,

"Mademoiselle Cora Pearl and the Earl of Arram."

As they came into the room every head was turned towards them.

Malvina thought it would be difficult to see a more distinguished looking couple.

Cora Pearl was not exactly beautiful in the classical sense, but there was no doubt she was a great personality.

As she embraced first her hostess, then a number of the other men and women present, sparks were flying out from her towards them.

If everyone present was covered in jewellery, Cora Pearl was obviously determined to exceed anything they could display.

She literally glittered from the top of her head to the soles of her feet.

With her sparkling eyes and smiling lips, Malvina could understand the gentlemen finding it difficult to look away from her.

"Many many happy returns of your birthday, dear

Cora," Blanche was saying. "We all have presents for you, but you can open them after dinner."

"How kind of you to think of me," replied Cora.

The sweeping glance she gave the people round her made it obvious she would have been surprised if they had not.

Dinner was then announced and Blanche led the way into the dining room which was next door.

The table had been decorated with white orchids as they were known to be Cora's special flower.

Everything arranged on the table was pure white with the exception of the candles which were pink and had shades speckled with diamante.

Everyone's name was written on a card in front of where they should sit.

Malvina quickly found the place for Celeste and as she started to sit down, she glanced at the name card of the gentleman on her right.

It was le Duc de Lavissé.

As she turned to see who was on her left, a guttural voice greeted her,

"I am Baron Wilhelm Von Herdorf, and as we have not been introduced, you must tell me your name."

With an effort Malvina remembered that she was now Celeste Doré and told him so.

"Then I am enchanted to meet you," said the Baron. "You must tell me why I have not met you before."

He spoke in rather a harsh manner, she thought, and it rather matched his appearance which seemed somewhat domineering.

He had thick dark hair, but was not a young man.

Although like many Germans he was fairly tall and

stoutly built, she thought there was something positively unattractive about him.

The Baron then started to speak to the woman on his other side and so Malvina turned towards the Duc de Lavissé.

She noticed, as she had not done before, that his left arm was in a sling.

He was good-looking and not, she felt, so obviously French as most of the other gentlemen were.

From where she was sitting she could see Charles Arram quite clearly.

He was sitting at the bottom end of the table beside Cora Pearl.

Their host and hostess, the Prince and Blanche were at the other end.

Now that she could see Charles Arram clearly at the table, Malvina realised he was in fact very handsome.

She could understand why women like Blanche and Cora Pearl were attracted to him.

In this party amongst so many dark-haired men he was outstanding.

His fair hair was brushed back tidily from a square forehead and his blue eyes accentuated his very English features.

It would have been impossible for anyone to think that he came from any other country.

He was smiling and talking animatedly to Cora and all the guests around him.

Malvina mused that she must be honest with herself and admit he was an exceedingly attractive young man.

As she continued to stare at him, the Duc broke into her thoughts,

"Is it possible, beautiful lady, that you are losing your heart to the Englishman who has stolen from us poor Frenchmen so many of these entrancing Goddesses you see seated round this table?"

Malvina gave a laugh.

"Are you speaking of Lord Arram?" she asked.

"Of course I am, mademoiselle. You will find if you are new to Paris, he is one of the subjects everyone talks about at every party."

Malvina laughed again.

"He must find that very flattering."

"I am sure he has all the flattery he requires sitting next to him at the moment," the Duc now remarked a little sourly. "Now, please, I would wish to ask why I have not seen you before in Paris."

"The answer is easy. I have only come to Paris for a short visit and our hostess was kind enough to invite me to dinner here tonight."

"Then let me say," the Duc replied, "that you will find you are very welcome in this City of beautiful women and undoubtedly you will become the new sensation that every man will wish to talk about."

Malvina gave a little cry.

"Oh no!" she exclaimed. "I have no wish to be a sensation at all. I just want to be an onlooker, which I am at the moment."

"Now you are being too modest, mademoiselle. Of course you will have to take part in this drama, charade, romance, or whatever you would call it and for which Paris is currently famous."

"I have heard that, but now I am actually here I find it is hard to believe I am not dreaming."

The Duc chuckled.

"We have all felt that at one time or another. But tell me why you have come to Paris, and why you have not been here before."

As she could not think of an immediate answer to his question, Malvina said quickly,

"I think it is my turn to ask questions, Monsieur le Duc. Why is your arm in a sling?"

The Duc looked down at it rather ruefully.

"I would like to tell you it is for a romantic reason and that I had to fight a duel. But actually, and I am rather ashamed to admit it, I fell off my horse!"

Malvina laughed loudly because his answer was so unexpected.

"I thought it would amuse you. It has been very painful, but I am pleased to say I am nearly myself again."

"What exactly happened?"

"I was taking my new horse over what I think now was a jump that was too high for him. He refused at the very last moment and to put it bluntly I went on and fell on some unpleasantly hard stones!"

"I am so sorry for you. I know how easy it is for that to happen with a young horse. My father very sensibly has had sand put down round the jumps when we train the newcomers."

"So you are a rider?"

There was the slightest hint of surprise in the Duc's voice that Malvina found amusing.

"Yes, I always ride when I am at home," she told him. "And I think nothing could be more enjoyable."

"That is what I think myself, mademoiselle, and I have been most frustrated these last few weeks not to be able to ride. That is one of the reasons why I came to Paris and also to see the best bone surgeon."

"How very sensible. I have always been told that the surgeons in Paris are better than any that are obtainable in London."

As she spoke Malvina knew that she had made a mistake.

Because she had been educated at St. Cloud no one would have suspected that she herself was of anything but French origin.

Before the Duc could speak and to cover up the slip she had just made, Malvina went on quickly,

"A friend of mine who was staying in England had a fall, and the English surgeon made a terrible mess of his injured leg."

"Then I am sorry for him, but I shall be riding again next week."

"You will have to be very careful for a little while," Malvina warned him.

"I realise that," replied the Duc. "But tell me about your horses and where you keep them."

"I think that you should tell me about yours first," Malvina countered evasively.

"My home is in Normandy and my château which is more like a fortified castle dates back to about 1200."

Malvina was interested.

"I have always wanted to see one of the very old châteaux," she sighed. "You are so lucky to own one."

"Unfortunately it is a very expensive proposition at the moment," the Duc added in a somewhat glum voice.

"Do you mean that you cannot afford to live in it?" enquired Malvina.

"It is not exactly that, but I cannot believe that at a party like this you are particularly interested in the troubles of a countryman."

"Having said so much about your château you have to tell me more," insisted Malvina.

"Very well," agreed the Duc. "It is a very large and ancient château and was at one time owned by a member of the Royal Family. His son gave it to my ancestor who was a warrior, a diplomat and a devotee of the arts."

"A rather exciting if overwhelming present."

"He was, as it happened, the most powerful man in all France next to the King. He owned a hundred and thirty châteaux and Baronies, six huge mansions in Paris and also kept his finger on the nation's pulse."

"I don't know what you mean by that, Monsieur le Duc, but indeed he must have been exceedingly clever to have kept so many things going at the same time."

"Apparently he was outstanding, and I only wish I could have lived in those days and met him."

"What happened to him?" enquired Malvina.

"When the Revolution came, my ancestor realised that if he was to remain alive he had somehow to win the approval of the Republicans."

"How could he do so?"

The Duc paused for a moment before answering,

"He ordered the villagers where his large and most important château was situated to demolish it!"

Malvina gave a cry.

"I don't believe it."

"Unfortunately it's true – they defaced the front, the towers, the entrance and the bridge over the moat."

"And that saved his life?" she asked breathlessly.

"They did not take him to the guillotine."

"It sounds an incredibly drastic way of pleasing the Revolutionaries," sighed Malvina.

"It was either that or his neck. To make himself even safer, my ancestor sold the furnishings and fittings of the château."

"I can hardly bear to think of it. It must have hurt him terribly."

"It ended the glorious career of my ancestor and it destroyed most of what was well known at the time as the *Palace of Kings*."

"So where do you live now, Monsieur le Duc?"

"In a château next to it. But what I want to do, if possible, is to restore the original château and make it once again one of the great beauties of Normandy."

"But of course you must do so," enthused Malvina.

The Duc smiled.

"It is a question of money. So you will understand I do not often come to Paris and I am rarely in the company of such delightful but exceedingly lovely ladies as are here tonight."

"I totally understand and therefore you must enjoy yourself whilst you are here."

"That is what I hope to do and I am sure of it now that I find I am sitting next to you."

Malvina giggled.

"That is an obvious compliment and you do make it sound as if I was fishing for it!"

"I would not suggest anything so rude and I assure you that I mean it. I am delighted, honoured and impressed by being seated on your right."

Malvina giggled again.

Then the Duc began to talk about his horses.

And as it was a subject on which she too was very fluent, there seemed to be much to say.

Unexpectedly the Baron on her other side piped up,

"Mademoiselle Doré, I am insulted that you have not spoken to me since we sat down to dinner!"

"I am sorry if I seem rude," said Malvina, "but I was talking about horses. It is a subject in which I am very interested so I am afraid I was carried away."

"If you want horses, I can give you any number of horses," the Baron proposed.

"So you too have horses," remarked Malvina, not understanding exactly what he meant.

"I am very rich and I have everything. If you are staying in Paris then you should have heard of me. I own several banks in France and most of the banks in Germany. So wherever I go I find I am very popular."

Malvina thought he was very conceited but it would be a mistake to be rude to him.

Instead she murmured,

"How interesting, I do not think I have ever met a banker before."

"Most bankers are not like me – as you will find to your satisfaction as we get to know each other better."

It passed through Malvina's mind that she had no wish to know him better.

The woman on the Duc's other side, was, Malvina had been told as she arrived, a successful actress.

She was talking to him in a somewhat confidential manner, so Malvina was then obliged to continue talking to the Baron.

She thought that he regarded her in an embarrassing manner.

"Do you live in Paris?" she asked the Baron.

"I have a house in the *Champs Élysées*," the Baron said, "but I only spend part of the year here. I come to stay only when there is someone around who I am particularly interested in."

"And who is she at the moment?" Malvina asked to keep the conversation going.

"I had not decided until I came here tonight, but I think, if you have no other commitment, beautiful lady, it shall be *you*."

Malvina could not think he was speaking seriously.

Yet as he moved a little closer to her and put out his hand to touch hers, she felt uncomfortable.

Fortunately, while she had been talking to the Duc, two courses had been served and now they had reached the third.

The food was delicious, but Malvina was finding it difficult to eat and talk simultaneously.

Therefore she had eaten very little by this stage of the dinner party.

Now looking round the table she saw that some of the guests seemed to be behaving very peculiarly.

Opposite her a man was kissing the naked shoulder of the lady on his right.

Further down the table there was a pretty woman with flaming red hair.

She wore a green dress which was embarrassingly *décolletée* and was sitting on the knee of the man beside her. Her arms were round his neck.

Malvina had noticed something odd while she was talking to the Baron.

The servants were filling up the glasses with wine the moment anyone had taken even a sip.

The champagne they had drunk before dinner had made everyone talk excitedly and all they had drunk since had only increased the noise around the table.

In fact there was so much chatter and laughter that it was impossible to hear everything the Baron was saying.

Malvina now turned round to talk to the Duc.

"It is a very noisy room and the German next to me has such a deep voice that I cannot hear what he is saying."

"I don't think you are missing very much," the Duc remarked, "but I am afraid this party will grow even noisier later on."

As if in answer to his words there was a shout of laughter and applause.

A chef had come though the door carrying a huge birthday cake and he set it down on the table in front of Cora Pearl.

Blanche bent forward to say,

"A happy birthday, dearest Cora, and you will see I have placed thirty-four candles on the cake for you to blow out."

"Thirty-four!" Cora exclaimed. "I am only *thirty* today as everyone knows."

"Oh no, Cora," replied Blanche. "You were always five years older than me and I was just twenty-nine last birthday, as darling Charles will remember."

"I am thirty!" Cora Pearl screamed. "*Thirty*!"

Taking up a spoon she knocked four candles off the top of the cake and they fell on the table.

Fortunately they were all extinguished before they could burn the expensive lace of the tablecloth.

"If Cora says she is thirty then that is what she is," Charles Arram shouted down the table.

His voice was so loud that it seemed to drown the other noise around him.

Then he raised Cora to her feet and handed her a knife to cut the cake.

"Blow out the candles first, darling," he told her.

She smiled at him – a bewitching smile, Malvina thought, and it would have been difficult for any man not to appreciate it.

Then she leaned forward and blew out the candles from the lower tier of the cake and then those on the top.

Now they were extinguished it was easy to see that on the cake there was a dancing figure of a naked woman.

It was obviously meant to represent Cora.

Yet even at a distance Malvina could see that it was a somewhat distorted image.

The dancer was fat and so were her legs.

She was not particularly well proportioned.

For a moment Malvina thought it was a mistake on the part of the chef.

Then, as she glanced at her hostess, she knew by the expression on Blanche's face that it was intentional.

Cora realised this at the same time.

"If that figure is meant to be me," she bawled, "it is an insult. And to show you what a bad likeness it is, I will dance for you on this table if someone will clear it."

She spoke angrily but the men round her cheered.

"That is what we all want, Cora. Come and show us what you can do."

"I *will* show you," Cora responded vigorously.

She started to undo the wide waistband of the over-decorated dress she was wearing.

Then Charles Arram held up his hand.

"I think," he announced, "that we should give Cora her presents first. As I have mine with me, it shall be the first."

He put his hand into his pocket and drew out what was obviously a jewel box.

Anyone who lived in Paris knew at once from the design on the lid that it had come from Oscar Mossin – the most expensive and admired jewellers in the whole of the City of Paris.

As Cora took it from Charles, all the women bent forward to see what it contained.

She opened the box gently and drew out a diamond bracelet that glittered in the light of the candles.

The women made a sound of admiration.

Then Cora screamed,

"That is not the bracelet I wanted! It was the other one!"

"The one that you wanted was unfortunately far too expensive for anybody who is not a rich Sultan or a King," Charles informed her, smiling.

"I can understand that," one of the men remarked.

"Well, I do not," cried Cora. "And on my birthday you should give me what I want – *not* this stuff."

She flung the bracelet as she spoke down onto the table in a gesture of disgust.

Then the sudden and surprised silence was broken as the Baron addressed Cora,

"I will give you what you want. You show me the bracelet you desire and it will be yours."

"Thank you! Thank you – " Cora began.

"Now you keep right out of this!" Charles shouted angrily. "It is nothing to do with you what I give Cora or what I cannot give her. I will ask you, Baron, to mind your own business."

"It *is* my business," the Baron howled out heatedly

rising to his feet. "If I want to give this gorgeous lady a diamond bracelet, there is nothing you can do to stop me."

"I am not certain about that," retorted Charles.

The two men were glaring at each other across the table when Blanche intervened,

"I will not permit fighting here at my table. If you want to fight, you must go outside. In the meantime let us all drink dear Cora's health on her birthday and wish her happiness. Also she has many other presents to open."

She held up her glass as she spoke.

As she was standing the gentlemen at the party rose a little unsteadily to their feet.

"Good Health!"

"Long Life!"

"God Bless You!"

Everyone made some apt remark before they drank, while Cora stood looking sulky and disagreeable.

Watching them, Malvina saw Charles pick up the bracelet she had thrown disdainfully onto the table and put it into his pocket.

Even as he did so the servants, as if at a signal from Blanche, removed the cake from the table.

Everyone then began to pile their presents in front of Cora.

For a moment Malvina thought that she was going to refuse to open them, but curiosity conquered her sulks.

She began to tear the coloured paper and ribbon off the presents.

The guests had started walking down the room to where Cora was seated to place their presents in front of her.

The Duc, however, had not moved and Malvina felt too shy to walk over alone to give Cora her present.

He turned towards her to suggest,

"Shall we go on somewhere a little quieter? I think they will now persuade Cora to dance as she promised she would and I doubt if you would find it enjoyable."

Even as he spoke, the doors at the far end of the room opened and there was a burst of spirited music from a band that was just inside the next room.

The Duc rose to his feet.

Without anyone apparently noticing them, he and Malvina slipped out of another door at far end of the room.

They were now in a passage which led to the hall and when they did reach it, the Duc lead the way upstairs.

On the first floor they passed a sitting room, but he did not stop. He merely walked on down the passage.

There was no sign of any servants and already the music was getting louder.

Someone was singing a popular song.

The Duc reached a door and opened it.

It led into a room that was partially in darkness.

Malvina followed him.

As he closed the door behind them, she saw there was an oil lamp on a table.

It was turned down very low and the Duc crossed the room to turn it up higher.

It revealed two comfortable armchairs in front of a fireplace which, as it was summer, was filled with flowers.

Then as Malvina looked to the end of the room, she saw to her surprise a large four-poster bed.

It was not unlike Blanche's, yet instead of being draped in blue, this one was draped in pink.

Now she could see clearly that the flowers in the room were all pink – there were several bowls of roses and carnations on several pieces of furniture.

Then as she looked round, she heard the Duc saying quietly,

"You may find me a little clumsy with my left arm and you might have to help me out of my coat, but I think, my lovely one, we shall enjoy ourselves far more here than we would below."

Malvina did not understand what he was saying.

She looked at him questioningly.

Then as he came a little nearer to her, he stretched out his right arm as if to put it round her.

Suddenly with a sense of shock, she realised what he meant.

She gave a scream of sheer horror and ran towards the door.

She reached it and tried to pull it open.

Without her realising it, the Duc had locked it when they came in.

She looked at him her eyes wide and frightened.

"Let me go!" she begged. *"Let me go!"*

The Duc, who had now slipped off his sling, stood looking at her in surprise.

"What can be upsetting you?" he asked.

"You should not have brought me here. I did not understand – " Malvina whispered somewhat incoherently.

"What did you not understand?" the Duc enquired. "You are very lovely and I want to tell you how adorable I find you."

Again Malvina gave a strangled cry.

"You do *not* understand. I have to go away now at once!"

The Duc sat down on one of the chairs.

"Now stop being hysterical," he counselled calmly, "and tell me what is upsetting you."

"It is all a mistake. I should not have come to this party, but I came for a special reason of my own."

"What reason?"

Malvina was still holding the handle of the door.

Now she released it and stood with her back to it.

"Please let me go," she pleaded. "As I have said, it is a mistake."

"A mistake for whom?"

"For *me*," Malvina answered.

"You came to the party knowing what it would be like. You must have known. If you are a friend of Blanche then you must be aware that she was giving a party because she is so very angry that Lord Arram had left her for Cora Pearl."

"I did not know that, but she let me come to the party because there was something I needed to find out."

"And what was that?"

"It is nothing that has anything to do with you, and when you suggested that we come away, I believed it was because you did not want me to see Cora Pearl dancing naked."

"I really wanted to have you on my own, Celeste. As it is a somewhat rowdy evening, I thought we would be happier together quietly up here – "

He paused before he added,

"I will try to make you happy."

"But I cannot stay here with you," she murmured. "Please *please* let me go."

"Of course, if that is what you want, I will not stand in your way."

Malvina gave a sigh of relief.

"Do you mean it?   Do you really mean it?"

"I have never yet forced myself on a woman who was unwilling. But shall I say that I am disappointed. Yet if that is what you wish, I will take you home."

"I can get home on my own – "

The Duc smiled.

"Looking as you do now, I do think it will be rather dangerous unless you have your own carriage and servants waiting for you outside."

Malvina was silent.

She had forgotten how she was dressed and what she looked like.

She was not so foolish as not to realise that if she tried to walk home through the streets as she was now, she would obviously be accosted.

As if the Duc understood without words what she was thinking, he suggested,

"Come on, I have a carriage outside and I will take you wherever you wish to go. But you must realise that I am very curious as to why, feeling as you do, you are here tonight with the most notorious *courtesans* in the whole of Paris."

"It was very stupid of me," Malvina mumbled in a small voice. "But I did have a good reason for coming."

She felt somehow that she must justify herself to the Duc, although there was really no need for her to do so.

He rose from where he was sitting and put his sling into the pocket of his coat.

"Can you manage without it?" Malvina asked him.

"I can manage, but I think, feeling as we both do now, it would be a mistake for you to touch me."

Malvina blushed and looked away.

"How could you have been so incredibly foolish as to get yourself into this mess?" the Duc asked her.

Malvina did not answer.

She merely stood to one side.

The Duc drew the key of the door out of his pocket and put it back into the lock.

Then he opened the door.

Now there was an overwhelming sound of music, voices and laughter.

"I think that we would be wise to leave by the side door. I know the way, but do be careful because it will be dark."

He did not wait for Malvina to answer.

Instead of turning right to go back the way they had come, he turned left.

There were some narrow steps which led down to the kitchen quarters.

There appeared to be nobody around and even the kitchen itself seemed to be empty of people.

The Duc opened a door at the end of a passage and then they were out of the house with steps leading up from the basement.

Now the night air was on Malvina's cheeks.

The Duc walked a little ahead of her to where at the front of the house there were a number of carriages.

There was one open as the hood was pulled back.

The Duc pulled open the door and helped Malvina inside.

His two servants were clustered with a number of others round the front of the house and they came running towards him.

"We were surely not expecting Your Grace to leave so early," one of them said.

"Enough is quite enough," the Duc replied. "We will take this lady home first then I am ready to go to bed."

"That's very sensible, Your Grace."

The Duc turned to Malvina who was already seated in the back of the carriage.

"Where are you staying?" he asked.

"9 *rue Faubourg St. Honoré*," she replied.

She thought for a second he looked surprised.

Yet it might have been because it was difficult to see him clearly.

He gave the order to the coachman and climbed in beside her.

The footman closed the door.

As they drove off, Malvina said,

"Thank you for being so kind. I am sorry if I have spoilt your evening."

"You have not spoilt it," answered the Duc. "But as you can imagine I remain very curious."

There was silence and then as the horses quickened their pace, Malvina added,

"Please just forget what happened tonight and that you have ever met me. We shall never meet again, so it will be easy for you."

"Why are you saying we shall never meet again?" the Duc now exploded. "I want to meet you again. I want to talk to you again and to save myself from worrying over a puzzle that I cannot find an answer to."

"When you go back to your horses, you will soon forget about me."

"Strangely enough I believe that will not happen.

Therefore I will call on you tomorrow and perhaps you will have luncheon or dinner with me. We can start as it were from the beginning, rather than coming in half way through a drama, not knowing what happened before or having the slightest idea of what will happen later."

Malvina laughed in spite of herself.

"Now you are making a big mystery out of it."

"What else can I make out of it?" the Duc asked. "I did not really want to come to the party tonight as I thought it would be very rowdy and my arm was hurting me. But perhaps it was fate that decided I should meet you."

"And perhaps it will be fate that will decide we will not meet again," retorted Malvina.

"Now I think you are being unnecessarily unkind. You must admit I have done exactly as you requested and brought you home."

"If you want to go back to the party, Monsieur le Duc, it will still be going on until the early hours of the morning."

The Duc chuckled.

"I expect they will have sorted themselves out by then. Although I would bet that tomorrow, despite what Charles Arram was saying, Cora will have the bracelet she desires so much from the Baron."

"How could she do such a thing?" Malvina asked. "He is such a horrible man."

"No one is horrible to Cora when they are as rich as the Baron!"

Malvina was silent as she thought it all sounded so unpleasant that she did not want to even think about it.

"You are right," the Duc counselled after a while. "It would be a big mistake for you to think about anything so crude and unsavoury."

"You are reading my thoughts," cried Malvina.

"I was rather surprised myself that I could do so and it is certainly something I would very much wish to do again."

"But it is something you must not do – "

By now they were passing through the *Place de la Concorde* and she looked up at the fountain.

"How can Paris be so beautiful?" she sighed.

"A great many have asked the same question. That is why so many men come to Paris to find the *Parisiennes* are as irresistible as the City itself."

"Is that what you have found?" Malvina asked him without thinking.

There was a pause before the Duc murmured,

"I thought the gates of Paradise would open for me, but you closed them very firmly."

There was silence and then Malvina persisted,

"Forget me. Please forget me and I am so sorry if I spoilt your evening. Thank you for being so very kind and bringing me home."

As they were talking the horses came to a standstill.

The footman climbed down to open the door.

The Duc followed him and helped Malvina down.

She had taken the key with her so as not to keep the servants up to let her in.

The Duc put out his hand and took it from her.

He opened the door, they both walked inside the house and he put the key down on a table.

It was very quiet and in total darkness except for one light flickering at the top of the stairs.

"Are you all right?" asked the Duc. "And is there someone to look after you?"

"Yes, I have someone to look after me and thank you for bringing me home."

She looked up at him as she spoke and he could see her eyes pleading with him in the light which came through the fanlight above the door.

He bent forward and his lips touched hers.

It was a very light kiss – the kiss a man might give a child.

Yet for a brief moment they both stiffened and it was impossible to breathe.

Then the Duc turned around and walked out of the open door and closed it behind him.

Without moving Malvina heard the carriage drive away.

Only when there was complete and absolute silence did she climb slowly up the stairs towards her bedroom.

CHAPTER FIVE

Malvina took a long time going to sleep.

When she awoke the sun was pouring through the sides of the curtains.

She got out of bed and had started to dress herself before Nanny came in.

"I didn't think you'd be awake so soon," mumbled Nanny. "I thought being so very late last night, you'd want your beauty sleep."

"I think we will go back to England this afternoon, Nanny," said Malvina unexpectedly

Nanny gave a cry.

"Oh, not this afternoon!"

"Why ever not?"

"Well, you said as how you were going to send the nurses to the theatre, and I thinks that the couple who looks after the old lady should go too. So I told them about it. And I thought as you weren't sure when we'd be leaving, we'd go to the theatre tonight."

Malvina did not speak and Nanny carried on,

"We've already booked all the seats at the *Théâtre des Variétés* which I hears is a really good show and I can tell you I'm looking forward to it."

"Then, of course, you must go, Nanny, and we will leave for England tomorrow. I will stay here tonight and look after her Ladyship."

"There's no need for that, Malvie. They've got it all arranged. The cook's sister who lives a little way down the road says she'll come in for the night with her husband, so it won't matter how late we are getting back."

As Malvina did not say anything, she continued,

"I expect you'll be going out with some friends and there's no need for you to worry about anything."

Malvina gave a sigh.

"No, of course not, Nanny, and I do want you to enjoy the theatre while you are here."

"I thought that you'd say that and it'll certainly be a change after being in the country for so long. I've almost forgotten what a stage looks like."

"You will remember soon enough when you get to the theatre."

When she had undressed last night, she had put the flamboyant gown and all the jewels that Blanche had lent her away in a drawer.

It was important that no one should see them, so after Nanny had left the room, she took the gown out and wrapped it up in some tissue paper.

Then she put it carefully in an empty dress-box and laid the jewels with it.

She had only just finished when Nanny came back into the room.

"Your breakfast is ready, Malvie, and I wondered why you hadn't come downstairs."

"I was just packing up something I have to take to one of my friends. I will see her after I have had breakfast. If you would like to go out shopping, Nanny, now is your opportunity."

"There are just a few things I'd like to take back," said Nanny, "things we can't buy in England, and the men servants in London asked me to bring them some funny postcards."

"I'm sure you will be able to do that, Nanny."

She picked up the dress-box and took it downstairs with her – just in case Nanny should be curious as to what was inside it.

Her breakfast was ready for her in the dining room and while the old manservant was waiting on her, she said,

"If anyone calls today and asks for Mademoiselle Celeste Doré, please say she has left and you have no idea where she has gone or when she will return."

She thought he looked surprised and she explained,

"She is a good friend of mine who is trying to avoid a man who is being particularly tiresome. She gave him this address so he could not find out where she actually is."

She realised from the expression on the man's face that he thought this was obviously a love affair and like all Frenchmen he accepted it as something quite ordinary.

An Englishman would have been far more curious.

However, Malvina was assured that if the Duc did ask for Mademoiselle Doré, he would receive the message she had left for him.

'I am sure that he has no intention of calling on me anyway,' she told herself.

Equally she could not help feeling that he would.

As soon as she had finished breakfast she picked up her dress-box and went out of the front door without telling anyone that she was leaving.

She had no wish to tell lies and yet she felt quite certain that if she stayed, Nanny would want to know what was in the dress-box.

She had not gone far before she found a fiacre and told the driver to take her to Blanche d'Antigny's house.

When she arrived it was nearly ten o'clock and she wondered if she was too early and Blanche would still be asleep.

She could just leave the box with only a message of gratitude.

But that would undoubtedly be rude and she hoped she would be able to see Blanche herself.

The door was opened by one of the footmen who looked at her and she realised that he did not recognise her.

Then she remembered that she was looking so very different from the way she had appeared last night.

As she began to speak, he gave an exclamation,

"You are the mademoiselle, who called on Madame yesterday morning!"

"Yes, I am. Will you be kind enough to tell her, if she is awake, that Lady Malvina Silisley would be pleased to see her for a few moments."

The footman took her into the same room where she had sat and waited yesterday morning – but today the room was very untidy.

There was coloured paper stacked on the chairs that must have been wrapped round the presents Cora Pearl had been given.

There were three broken fans on a table and several handkerchiefs and scarves which had obviously been left by the guests were on another chair.

Malvina did not have to wait long.

The footman soon came back to say that Madame was awake and would be delighted to see her.

Malvina was taken up the stairs and into Blanche's beautiful blue bedroom.

Blanche was lying back against some pillows, her champagne-coloured hair falling down over her shoulders.

Even without any make-up, she looked exceedingly attractive.

"Good morning, Celeste," she called out as Malvina entered. "What happened to you last night? I looked for you and found that you and the Duc had disappeared."

"He took me home," replied Malvina, "as I thought that I had seen everything that I wanted to see."

Then quickly before Blanche could speak, she said,

"I have brought back your gown and the jewels and I want to thank you a million times for lending them to me. And for allowing me to come to such an extraordinary and unusual party."

Blanche laughed.

"I knew it would seem extraordinary and unusual to you. It is actually a good thing you left when you did!"

Malvina raised her eyebrows.

"Why?" she asked.

"Because Charles and the Baron had a furious row. It amused most of the guests, but I think it would have shocked you."

"Why particularly?"

"Charles told the Baron to mind his own business and that as he was looking after Cora Pearl and the Baron had no right to offer her any presents whilst she was under his protection."

Malvina was listening intently and she asked a little nervously,

"I suppose that is correct etiquette?"

"It is more or less one of the strict unwritten laws," replied Blanche lightly. "But as Cora stole Charles away from me, I could not help finding it all very amusing."

Malvina could see her point.

"What happened then?" she enquired.

"The two men raged at each other using especially unpleasant language, but I am thankful to say they avoided a duel."

"I am glad to hear it, although I am certain Charles would have beaten the Baron."

"I am not that sure. The Baron has won quite a few duels and he is, as it so happens an excellent pugilist."

Malvina gave an exclamation of surprise.

Then she asked,

"And what happened eventually?"

"Cora, still pretending she was thirty and not thirty-four," Blanche said a little spitefully, "took Charles away, making it clear to everyone, including me, that he belonged to her. At the same time, when he was not looking, she gave the Baron an encouraging smile and a squeeze of his hand that told him that she was ready to accept the bracelet whenever he was prepared to offer it to her!"

Malvina gave a cry.

"Oh, how could she do such a thing? He is such a horrible man."

"But very rich," added Blanche, "and that of course means more to Cora than anything else."

"I expect you know that Charles Arram should not spend money as he is doing now. His father is striving to keep the house and estate in good order, but it is a struggle and that is exactly why my father wanted to help him by persuading me to marry Charles."

"Now you have seen Charles, are you prepared to take him on," enquired Blanche, "and to make him behave as a correct Englishman should?"

Malvina shook her head.

"As I told you, I was determined before I came here not to agree to an arranged marriage. Now I am even more determined than I was before. I will never marry anyone unless I am in love with him and he is in love with me."

Blanche clapped her hands.

" Bravo, *ma chèrie*! You are so right. That is just as you should be feeling at your age and I can only hope your dreams will come true."

She gave a little sigh before she added,

"It is just what I dreamt myself when I was young. Although I have been enamoured and happy with quite a number of gentlemen, I have always known that what they feel for me would not last for ever."

There was a distinct sadness in her voice that made Malvina exclaim,

"I am sorry – *so* sorry."

Blanche chuckled.

"No one listening to you would believe that anyone need be sorry for me at the moment. I am one of the great successes of Paris and, believe it or not, there is a whole battalion of distinguished gentlemen ready to take Charles Arram's place."

"I can well believe it – you are *so* beautiful."

"It is because I give them so much of the happiness and amusement that they cannot find anywhere else. My Prince whom you met last night has waited five years for me. So he is very happy."

"But for how long?" queried Malvina.

She thought as she spoke that perhaps the question was rather rude.

Yet she was so curious.

Blanche made a gesture with her hands.

"It can only be answered by the Goddess of Love herself, and I hope it will be for a long time, but there may be another Cora Pearl waiting to entice him away when I least expect it!"

It was a scenario that Malvina had never anticipated could happen to anyone as lovely as Blanche.

Now she was quite certain in her own mind that the exquisite *courtesan* had really been in love with Charles.

There was nothing further she could say, so after a little pause, she enquired,

"Did Cora Pearl really dance last night as she said she was going to do?"

Blanche gave a long laugh and it swept away what Malvina thought was the pain in her green eyes.

"She danced to the band – just to show us that she was more beautiful than the effigy on her birthday cake."

Malvina did not like to ask the obvious question but Blanche added as if she had done so,

"She was nearly naked and there is no doubt at all that her figure is as exquisite as everyone in the room told her it was."

Malvina felt glad that she had not been there.

Again Blanche understood and remarked,

"I am very grateful to the Duc for taking you away. You are too young for what happened here last night and it is something you must forget all about when you return to England."

"I am going back home tomorrow."

"That is most sensible of you and I am certain you will be able to persuade your father that Charles Arram is not the right husband for you."

"It is going to be difficult, but because Papa loves me, I am sure he will understand."

"I, too, am sure he will," agreed Blanche.

Malvina rose to her feet.

"I can only thank you again, madame, for being so kind. And if you come to England I would like you to stay at my home and see my father's marvellous horses."

"I will certainly think about it, but I have a feeling that when you return to England, it will be wise as a Social *debutante* to forget you have ever met Blanche d'Antigny or been introduced to Cora Pearl!"

Malvina gave a little laugh.

"I will never forget it, but I will be wise enough not to talk about it."

"That is very sensible of you. Goodbye, *ma chèrie*, and God bless you. I hope you will find a man who will love you as you want to be loved and that you will marry him and be happy ever afterwards."

As she spoke she put her arms round Malvina and kissed her.

"Thank you, thank you so much, madame, and I too shall pray that you will always be happy."

"I do hope that your prayers will be answered."

Malvina walked towards the door.

Then she turned back to have a last look at Blanche.

She looked exquisitely lovely lying in the blue bed against the lace-edged pillows.

Malvina waved her hand as Blanche murmured,

"*Au revoir.*"

Then she was hurrying downstairs into the hall.

When she reached it, the two footmen were taking in large baskets and bouquets of flowers – obviously sent to Blanche by the guests she had entertained the previous evening.

Malvina had been wise enough to keep the fiacre.

As she stepped into it she saw a carriage driven by two well-bred horses with smartly liveried servants on the box draw up behind her.

As she drove off she could not help looking back curiously.

She wondered who was calling on Blanche so early in the morning.

And she was not surprised to see it was the Prince.

He looked very smart as he walked up the steps that led to the front door.

'I am certain that Blanche will be very happy with him,' she mused.

At the same time she could not help realising that he was very much older and not nearly as good-looking as Charles Arram.

As she drove on she found herself going over in her mind exactly what she would say to her father.

She was very sure that he would be shocked when he learnt that Charles was busy spending money he could not afford on Cora Pearl.

Yet would he agree that Charles was not the right husband for her, whatever the Marquis might feel about it?

She could not be sure of the answer.

Equally Malvina was quite sure her father would be extremely angry with her for going to Paris on her own.

And he would dislike the whole idea of her seeking the assistance of Blanche d'Antigny.

'But I have proved my point,' Malvina surmised, 'and after all this he cannot force me to marry Charles who anyway quite obviously has no wish to marry me.'

But she knew she was still nervous about having to

tell her father how she had taken the matter into her own hands.

However, there was one episode in the drama that she certainly would not tell him about.

That was how the Duc had taken her into the pink bedroom and what had occurred there – it would make her father very angry indeed.

Of course it was all her fault for not realising that, looking like a *cocotte*, she was quite obviously going to be treated like one.

Then Malvina found herself pondering as she had before she fell asleep of the kiss the Duc had given her in the hall.

She had never been kissed before, although quite a number of men had tried to do so, either in the gardens of Devonshire House or in some empty reception room when she was attending a private ball.

She had always believed that a kiss was a sensation too intimate to be wasted on a man who meant nothing to her.

Now she told herself that she would never see the Duc again –

Yet she had the uncomfortable feeling it would be impossible to forget his kiss.

It had not been what she expected.

Nor had she thought that she herself would feel like responding to him.

Yet when his lips did touch hers, she felt a strange feeling she had never felt before move through her breasts.

Even as she had become aware of it, he had left her. He had just walked out of the door without looking back.

Only when she was lying in bed and could not sleep did she feel again that strange unaccountable feeling.

She wanted to tell herself it was what everyone felt when they were first kissed.

But she knew it was untrue – what had happened to her was something quite different.

So different that she was now frightened she would not be able to forget it.

'The sooner I return to London, the better,' she told herself, as she drove through the *Place de la Concorde*.

The fountains were brilliant in the sunshine and she wanted to think only of Paris and how lovely it was.

Instead she was standing once again in the darkness of the hall.

The Duc had bent forward when she looked up at him and his lips touched hers.

She paid the fiacre driver when she arrived back at her cousin's house.

She gave him a large tip and he responded,

"*Merci beaucoup*, mademoiselle."

She went into the house, opening the door with the key she had taken with her last night.

The house itself seemed very quiet, but she could hear voices in the kitchen.

She thought the staff would all be talking excitedly about what they would see tonight at the theatre.

She walked into the room where she had found the newspapers that told the stories of Cora Pearl.

She now no longer wanted to look at them.

She had met Cora Pearl.

And she had seen not only Blanche, but many other of the infamous *cocottes*.

It was a world she could never belong to.

Now she did not want to think about it all anymore, only to forget what had happened.

She could still see the fury on Charles Arram's face when the Baron had offered to give Cora Pearl the bracelet he could not afford.

She could hear the rather spiteful note in Blanche's voice, when she had insisted that Cora was thirty-four not four years younger as she claimed.

The *cocottes* might indeed be glamorous and look very different from any woman she had ever met.

Yet they suffered just as ordinary people do from jealousy and resentment.

'I do want to go back home,' Malvina murmured.

She felt like a child wanting to run to her mother for comfort.

However, she and Nanny would leave for England tomorrow.

She must tell the butler to notify the courier whom she was paying to stay in Paris until she called for him.

She ate her luncheon alone in the dining room.

When she had finished Nanny came in to say,

"I'm just going out to do a bit of shopping, Malvie. One of the nurses wants to come with me, but we won't be away long. Are you going to stay here now or will you be joining your friends?"

"I expect I shall be seeing my friends," she replied rather mournfully.

"That'll be very nice for you, and mind you fix up something for yourself tonight. I don't want you staying here alone."

"I expect that I will be able to arrange something, Nanny."

110

She knew it would worry Nanny if she thought she was having a lonely evening all by herself.

"We're all very grateful to you and that's the truth," Nanny rambled on. "It'll be something for me to talk about when I gets back to England, you can be sure of that."

Malvina laughed.

"It will make them jealous and if you say too much in the country, all our staff will go to London for the bright lights!"

"They're not as stupid as that, Malvie, they knows where their bread's buttered. Your father looks after them real well."

Malvina knew this to be true.

Her father was always most generous to his staff. He always took care of them, besides paying them well.

'It is what I shall have to do when I have a house of my own and am married,' pondered Malvina.

That thought made her aware once again of the way Charles had been so possessive over Cora Pearl.

'How could I ever marry a man who is only content with women like those last night?' she asked herself.

She realised, although she tried not to think about it, she had been shocked at the way the men and women had been behaving at dinner.

She could see in her mind all too clearly the girl in green sitting on a man's knee and the woman opposite her putting her arms round another's neck and kissing him.

She just could never imagine anything like this ever taking place at home.

She could only hope that even a young man such as Charles would find it boring and rather vulgar after a time.

But that would be no reason at all for him to wish to

settle down to matrimony or to behave as his father and her father wished him to do.

Despite every effort of hers not to, Malvina found herself thinking once again of the kiss the Duc had given her in the hall.

On an impulse she jumped up from where she was sitting and ran up to her bedroom.

She put on a hat which matched the very pretty blue and white dress she was wearing.

Then she slipped downstairs without saying a word to Nanny or anyone else.

Once again she could hear a great deal of chatter in the kitchen.

She let herself quickly out of the front door locking it behind her.

She walked down the hill and into the road that led to the *Rue Royale* in which was the Madeleine.

The Madeleine was a famous Church that Malvina had visited several times when she was at the Finishing School in St. Cloud.

It had been pointed out to the girls as one of the most interesting and beautiful Churches in the City.

Because it was nearby, Malvina knew now that she wished to go there and say a prayer.

It was, she thought, going to be a simple prayer – one which should receive an answer as soon as she had finished praying.

She duly recognised that she should not be walking alone in Paris. It was something that her father would have been most annoyed at her doing.

But it was only a short distance to the Madeleine.

She walked swiftly, not stopping to look in the shop

windows or to loiter.

In fact, as she hoped, no one showed any interest in her.

She reached the Church safely, walked up the steps and in through the great West door.

There was a scent of incense and an atmosphere she had known before of generations of faith which one could feel as soon as one entered the building.

Impulsively she then turned and hurried towards the Chapel that stood just inside the West door.

She had never prayed there before, but she recalled the teacher who had taken her and a number of other pupils around the Madeleine nearly a year ago, saying,

"What is considered very unusual in the Madeleine is the Chapel of Saint Joseph. He is the Saint of Marriage because he was married to the Virgin Mary. But very few Churches remember him and that is why it is unique for the Madeleine to have a Chapel dedicated only to him."

As Malvina went towards it she could see that there was a large number of candles burning in front of the altar.

There were also flowers laid at the foot of it.

She thought there must be some special reason for them. Perhaps it was the day that Saint Joseph had been canonized that was being commemorated.

There were a few people kneeling in front of the altar.

Having lit a candle, she knelt down to pray.

Almost without her willing it or thinking about it, she asked fervently in her prayer that she would completely forget the disturbing kiss she had received from the Duc.

It became, although she did not intend it to be, a long and protracted prayer.

All the time she was kneeling and praying she was again conscious of the same ecstatic feeling that had risen within her breasts.

'How can I go through my life always thinking of this one kiss from the Duc,' she entreated in her prayers, 'and maybe comparing his kiss with any other kisses I may receive in the future?'

Then she forced herself not to think about his kiss, but to pray.

But somehow the feeling remained there – it was not spirited away from her as she had hoped it would be.

It must have been perhaps twenty minutes or half-an-hour later that she rose from her knees.

She moved from the Chapel back towards the West door and since she had entered the Madeleine, the central doors had been closed.

She therefore walked to the smaller door at the side.

She was pulling it open, but the door was heavy.

She then became aware that there was a man behind her who had put out his hand to assist her.

Between them they managed to open the door.

As they did so Malvina just looked up to thank the stranger who had helped her.

She gave a loud gasp.

It was the Duc de Lavissé.

He looked at her as if surprised that she had not passed quickly on.

Then he gave an exclamation,

"Celeste!"

Malvina walked through the door and he followed her.

They stood in front of the West door.

"Why are you here?" he asked. "I called at your house this morning and was told you had left Paris without leaving an address."

"I am going soon."

The Duc smiled.

"That gives me a chance to talk to you as I wish to do. My carriage is below and I will take you wherever you want to go. But I think first that we should drive along the Seine so that I can talk to you."

It flashed through Malvina's mind that she ought to refuse and somehow escape from him.

But before she could think of what she should say, he had taken her arm and was helping her down the steps.

His carriage was waiting by the gates.

She reflected how last night they had driven away from the party without anyone being aware they had gone.

The Duc helped her onto the back seat.

As the footman closed the door he told him to drive along the Seine.

As he sat down beside Malvina, he sighed,

"How could you possibly think of leaving the City of Paris without visiting the Seine?"

The way he spoke made her laugh.

"I don't suppose the Seine would have noticed my absence," she quipped.

"But I should," answered the Duc. "How could you have sent me away this morning in despair?"

Malvina did not answer and he carried on,

"I went into the Madeleine to pray that somehow I should be able to find you. I prayed to St. Anthony who is the special Saint for things that are lost, and he could not have answered me more quickly or more effectively!"

Malvina felt that there was nothing she could say.

After a moment the Duc enquired,

"Tell me why you were there too?"

It was a question she had not expected.

Malvina turned her face away and yet she was very conscious that there was a faint blush on her cheeks.

Once again, as he had done last night, the Duc read her thoughts.

"You were praying that you would be able to forget that I had kissed you. How could you do anything so cruel and so unkind?"

"It would not be cruel if we never met each other again."

"Do you really believe, Celeste, that you could go away and forget me and how we met in such strange and unusual circumstances?"

Malvina could not answer, so she just looked away from him.

There was a silence until he commented,

"Now I can see you clearly without all that stuff on your face and I realise that you were wearing a wig last night, I do not believe you are French! I am almost sure that you are English."

"Stop guessing about me," insisted Malvina, "and please let me go home. You know very well that I should not have been at that party last night and I want to forget all about it more than anything else."

"I want you to forget the party but not *me*," the Duc replied. "Please answer my question. Are you English and not French as you were pretending to be last night?"

He spoke the last sentence in English.

To Malvina's astonishment his English was good and he did not appear to have any trace of a French accent.

"You speak English!" she exclaimed.

"It is not surprising as my mother was English. But

your French is excellent and, of course, your disguise was indeed a clever one. I presume that Blanche arranged it for you."

"You are guessing far too much," Malvina told him in a small voice. "Please, please, Monsieur le Duc, I have to forget you. So just take me home."

"You know as well as I do," the Duc stated firmly, "it is impossible for me to forget you – or for you to forget me. So let us enjoy each other's company. Stop arguing and just be *yourself*."

Malvina did not speak for a moment and then she said,

"If I tell you the truth you will be shocked and that will only make things worse than they are already."

"As far as I am concerned you did nothing wrong. Last night you deceived me into behaving in a way I would not have behaved if you had looked as you look now. But I took you home when you asked me to do so, and I think you might even say that I behaved like a perfect English gentleman!"

Despite herself Malvina laughed.

"I grant you that is exactly what you did, and as I said at the time, thank you for being so kind to me."

The Duc sat back on the leather seat.

"Now tell me the whole story. I think I am entitled to hear it. I can only promise you that nothing you tell me will ever be repeated to anyone, even under torture."

"I don't think that anyone will torture you on my behalf," smiled Malvina. "But it is a story I am not very proud of. I would so much prefer just to thank you again and hope that when I return to England, as I intend to do very soon, you will forget me."

"Do you really think that is possible? For one thing for the rest of my life, I would be dying of curiosity – "

He put out his hand and laid it on hers.

"Just be more sensible, Celeste, if that really is your name. We have enjoyed a strange and unusual adventure together and you cannot now throw me out as if I was of no consequence."

In the depths of her heart Malvina knew this to be true.

After a moment she enquired,

"How is it possible when I was quite certain that I would never see you again that we should meet in such an extraordinary way?"

"We both thought at the same time," the Duc told her quietly, "that we would take our troubles – and mine was a very big one – to a Power greater than ourselves."

He smiled before he went on,

"You must admit that my prayer to find you again was answered immediately and I shall express my gratitude to St. Anthony at the first opportunity.

"Now you must tell me just why you were praying to forget me and that I had kissed you."

Again because she felt he had read her thoughts, Malvina blushed.

"That is the real truth, is it not? You were finding it hard to forget what you felt when my lips touched yours. I, for my part, lay awake thinking about it *all* last night."

Malvina was still looking ahead without seeing the scenery they were passing.

"Tell me," he asked, "how many men have kissed you before?"

"No one," she murmured. "No one, except you."

"That is exactly what I thought. Yet how could I imagine for one instant that that is what I would find at one of Blanche's notorious parties?"

"Are they always like that?"

"Some are better and some are worse, but whatever they are like, a very lovely girl from England who I would suspect is not much older than eighteen, should *not* have been invited."

"It was not Blanche's fault," said Malvina quickly. "I asked her to help me and she thought that the best way she could do so was to let me be a guest at the party which she gave last night."

"And how did that help you particularly?"

She felt his questions were becoming too difficult to answer.

"Let me say I did find out what I wanted to know, and that was – why I was glad when you suggested – we went somewhere quiet."

She hesitated a little over her words and again she was blushing.

There was a faint smile hovering on the Duc's lips as he watched her.

"Only a Englishwoman with a complexion just like yours could blush so exquisitely. It is a long time since I have seen a woman blush."

"If you were being polite," complained Malvina, "you would pretend not to notice it."

"I adore you when you blush," he sighed. "And let me tell you, you are a million times more beautiful today as a lovely English girl that you were yesterday as a very convincing French *cocotte*."

Unexpectedly he then demanded,

"Take off your hat."

It was something Malvina wanted to do anyway as she never wore one when she was at home.

Without thinking about it she obeyed him.

The sun touched the curls of her golden hair.

She then threw her hat down onto the seat opposite them.

"Now I am being so unconventional in an English way. You have a very bad effect on me."

"Actually, as we have already said, I think I can be praised for my performance. But I am still waiting for you to tell me exactly why you are here in Paris and apparently unchaperoned."

"It's not true. I thought I told you last night that I have brought my Nanny with me. I only went alone to the Church because she had gone shopping and I was finding it difficult to forget last night."

"What you are actually saying, is you are finding it difficult to forget my kiss, and let me add firmly that I have no intention of allowing you to forget me as well!"

After a moment Malvina turned her face to look at him.

"You cannot expect to remember me, Monsieur le Duc, after I have gone back to England," she persisted.

The Duc smiled at her.

"There is nothing to prevent me coming to England and staying with my mother's relations. It is just no use running away, Celeste. We have found each other and it is going to be very difficult for either of us to escape."

Malvina did not answer and he added,

"Very well. There is no need to hurry, what do you want to talk about, if it is not ourselves?"

Malvina gave a little laugh.

"That is easy. Let's talk about horses and I have not asked you yet, how is your arm?"

CHAPTER SIX

The Duc did not answer her.

They were by now driving alongside the Seine.

He suddenly bent forward and told the coachman to draw in between the next two trees.

As they did so he suggested to Malvina,

"We will walk down the bank and you shall see the Seine from its own level."

It was something that she had wanted to do when she was at the Convent.

But the nuns had always insisted the girls should only walk along the Seine on the pavement by the side of the main road.

The Duc helped Malvina down the steps and then they were on a level with the river as it flowed swiftly past them.

There were several huge barges moving on the river and one or two smaller boats.

They stood looking at the scene in silence.

Then the Duc said,

"I always feel when I come here that the river Seine is like one's life. There are interesting things happening on either side, but there is always tomorrow and the days after when there will be more fascinating sights to see than those that are here at the moment."

Malvina smiled.

"I like that idea. I have never thought of myself as

moving on a river before. But if it has to be one, I would like it to be the Seine."

"I always find it very romantic and most inspiring. I seldom visit Paris without coming here."

He drew her towards a seat as he was speaking.

They sat down watching the passing river traffic.

Then the Duc asked her,

"Have you seen Blanche today? I rather suspected you would take back her gown and her jewellery."

Malvina looked at him in surprise.

"How did you know that she had lent them to me?"

"Seeing you as you are now, I could hardly imagine that you would have bought that gown, attractive though it was. Also, I had a suspicion when we first met that I had seen the diamond necklace you were wearing on Blanche."

"She was being very kind to me."

Malvina spoke almost as if the Duc was criticising Blanche.

"Blanche is kind to everyone," he told her. "It is one of her most charming attributes."

A thought suddenly occurred to Malvina.

Because he was so familiar with Blanche, he must have been in love with her.

Somehow the idea upset her although she could not think why.

Then the Duc said quietly,

"*No*, you are wrong!"

"You are reading my thoughts again," she cried.

"At least it saves you the obvious embarrassment of speaking them out loud!"

"I would not have been – so impertinent."

She stumbled a little over the last word, as if she was uncertain as to how she could express what she meant.

"I will tell you about Blanche," the Duc suggested, "because I think it will interest you."

Malvina did not answer and he began,

"Her real name was Marie-Ernestine Antigny and her father, as you might have been told, was a carpenter in a little town near Bourges."

Malvina did not reveal that she had already heard about Blanche from the Comte.

The Duc continued.

"Her father ran away with a local woman and some years later Madame Antigny went to Paris in search of him. While she was here the two children she brought with her died and she sent for Marie-Ernestine to come and join her.

"Madame Antigny had, while she had been in Paris, started to do sewing and housework for some distinguished families, my own amongst them. Blanche was nine at the time and I was eleven. Because I was an only child I found it very amusing to play with a little girl in the garden of our house in the *Champs Élysées*."

"She must have been a very pretty little girl."

"She was indeed pretty and charming, but Madame Antigny was also working for the Marquis de Gallifet. He sent Marie-Ernestine to school at the *Couvent des Oiseaux*, a Convent School where she learnt poise and good manners as well as all the other subjects on the curriculum."

Malvina was finding all this particularly interesting.

She turned herself sideways so that her eyes were on the Duc, as he carried on,

"The only subjects Blanche really enjoyed were her geography, which gave her a longing for adventure and the

Holy Scripture. Had it not been for the untimely death of the Marquis de Gallifret, she might have become a nun."

"A nun!" exclaimed Malvina.

She could not image Blanche as a nun.

"When I was just nineteen," the Duc continued with the story, "my mother insisted that I should attend Oxford University."

Malvina gave a cry.

"So you were educated in England."

"Partly, and of course I stayed with all my mother's relations. I enjoyed riding their horses and meeting their friends. In fact I found England really delightful."

It seemed to Malvina strange that the Duc should be half English and had attended Oxford.

At the same time it explained why he spoke English so perfectly.

She had considered from the very first moment she had seen him that he did not seem to be in the least like the other Frenchmen at the party.

"When I came back to France," the Duc went on, "I was twenty-one and Blanche was already a great celebrity. She had been quite a success on the stage and she was also undoubtedly one of the most important and sought after of all the participants in the *Beau Monde*."

The enthusiasm in his voice made Malvina draw in her breath.

Now, she thought, he was going to tell her how he had fallen in love with Blanche.

Although she knew the revelation was inevitable, it was something she decidedly did not want to hear.

"Naturally as soon as I was back in Paris I renewed my acquaintance with dear Blanche. She took me under her wing as if she was the sister she had seemed to be when we were children."

"What do you mean, she took you under her wing?" asked Malvina in a small voice.

"She knew that I wanted to enjoy myself and so she introduced me to the world which she now ruled. And she protected me."

"How? In what way?"

"She introduced me to the *courtesans*, who were, of course, her friends and her rivals, but made it quite certain that I avoided those who would extort too much from their lovers – like Cora Pearl."

Malvina was finding it hard to understand what had happened.

"In many ways I suppose Blanche mothered me. There was always a room for me in any house she owned. That was why, although I could see that it surprised you, I knew how we could escape last night through the back of the premises."

He continued talking about Blanche and the parties he had been to.

He was looking at the Seine, so he did not see the expression of relief in Malvina's eyes.

She was glad, so glad that she felt as if the sunshine itself was brighter.

The Duc had *not* been Blanche's lover.

"Now that I have told you about myself, and how grateful I am to Blanche," the Duc finished, "and now even more so after last night as she seated me next to you."

"Do you think," she asked, "that Blanche wanted us to become friends or was she perhaps just protecting me from some of the men at the party?"

"If I am honest," replied the Duc, "I think Blanche

was thinking of me and how much I should enjoy meeting you."

There was no answer to that.

As Malvina did not speak, he rose to his feet.

"I am now taking you back, because I have to see my surgeon later this afternoon. But I would like to take you out to dinner and will pick you up at eight o'clock."

Malvina looked at him.

"I don't think that I ought to dine with you."

The Duc smiled.

"What you mean is – without a chaperone. Well, I have no intention of supplying one, because I want to talk to you. I will take you somewhere very quiet, where no one will see us and the food is delicious."

He was looking at her as he spoke.

Her eyes fell beneath his.

"I might have an engagement – "

"If you have, you must cancel it. I want to talk to you and I have already planned that I will bring a picture of my château to show you."

He gave a wry smile before he added,

"The 'château of dreams' that may never come true, but I go on hoping."

"I would love to see the picture."

"Perhaps it would be possible for me to show you the château itself before you return to England."

They were walking as he spoke back towards the steps that would lead them up to the road.

Malvina did not answer him.

She felt even more certain than she had been before that she must return to England tomorrow.

But she wanted to go on talking to the Duc.

She wanted to have dinner with him.

But it would only make it more difficult than it was already to forget him.

The Duc helped her into the carriage and told the coachman to drive back to the *Faubourg St. Honoré.*

"I am feeling a little embarrassed," he admitted, as the horses started off, "as I have been talking about myself when I should really have been talking about you. But you are being very evasive, so I did not like to press you."

"I have enjoyed hearing about Blanche," Malvina said truthfully. "And I would really love to see the picture of your château."

"I have a feeling that you will be full of brilliant ideas as to what I should do and what I should not do with my château. The only difficulty is I cannot afford, for the moment, to put them into operation.

"I have a large number of relations and they have to come first. Just as in your country, the head of the family is responsible for the well-being of every one of them."

"It must be a hard tie for you, when you are longing to spend all you can afford on rebuilding your château."

"At least I can imagine it as it was. As you will see from the picture I will be bringing which shows it when it was the *Palace of Kings.*"

They were nearing the *Faubourg St.Honoré* when he said,

"Perhaps I made a mistake this afternoon in talking too much. I should have been telling you how lovely you look and asking what you are planning for yourself."

Malvina laughed lightly.

"Because you are so able to read my thoughts, you very likely know the whole story without my putting it into words."

"I adore listening to your voice, Celeste. So many women have hard shrill voices, but yours is perfect. It is like the softness and beauty of flowers which I know you love as I do."

"Of course I love flowers," enthused Malvina, "and as Blanche was receiving enormous bouquets this morning from her many admirers, I felt almost jealous!"

"So you *have* been to see Blanche this morning, I thought you would have."

"I was naturally returning the lovely necklace you recognised."

"You don't need diamonds to enhance your beauty, but I would love to give them to you."

Malvina giggled.

"You have already forgotten that the château must come first before you can think of giving flowers let alone diamonds to anyone!"

"There can be exceptions to every rule!"

"I think," counselled Malvina, "that you would still feel in your heart of hearts that it would be cheating."

The Duc laughed as the horses came to a standstill outside the house.

"I will call for you at exactly eight o'clock," he said as he was helping her out of the carriage. "And I shall be counting the minutes until I can see you again."

"That is a very pretty speech, Monsieur le Duc," Malvina responded mockingly. "But I just don't believe a word of it!"

"We will talk about it again this evening."

He made no attempt to enter the house.

The footman had already rung the bell and the door had been opened by the old butler.

The Duc climbed back into his carriage and when it drove off, Malvina waved goodbye to him.

Then as she walked inside, the butler remarked,

"That be a fine looking gentleman who has brought you back, my Lady."

"He gave me a lift from my friends," Malvina said quickly, "and I will be dining with them again tonight."

She saw that this story pleased the old servant, but equally she disliked telling lies.

Yet she knew if Nanny was suspicious that she was dining alone with a gentleman, she might make a fuss.

What was more when they returned to England, she would undoubtedly tell her father and he would certainly be annoyed.

'I am getting very involved,' thought Malvina, 'and it is a good thing I am going back to England tomorrow.'

Equally she realised that she did not want to go.

She wanted to see more of the Duc.

But what was the use?

The kiss she could not forget had meant nothing to him.

He was just prepared to amuse himself with her.

When he did return to the country and his beloved château, he would not think of her again.

She told herself that she was not taken in by all his many compliments.

All Frenchmen paid women elaborate compliments.

They meant as little as an Englishman saying a girl was 'a good sport'.

She went to the sitting room before going upstairs.

She realised she was again feeling, because she had

been with the Duc, that intense, strange and ecstatic feeling she had felt when he kissed her.

'I really must not fall in love, I must *not*,' she cried almost frantically to herself.

Even as she murmured the words, she knew that it was too late.

Foolishly, because she could not help herself, she had fallen in love with a man who would never love her in the same way.

He had believed her to be a *courtesan* like Blanche.

Now he found it amusing to talk to an English girl.

He had actually apologised for being deceived by the way Blanche had dressed her to look like a *cocotte*.

Yet he would, when she had departed, forget her immediately.

'Why, after all,' she now asked herself, 'should he do anything else?'

*

Nanny was packing her clothes into her trunk when she finally went upstairs.

"Oh, there you are, Malvie. I'd heard you'd gone out and I hope you've fixed up with your friends to dine with them tonight."

"There is someone calling for me at eight o'clock. So just enjoy yourself, Nanny, and don't worry about me."

"I was just thinking, that you haven't bought much since you've been in Paris. I thought maybe you could buy an extra gown or two for you to wear in London."

"It is easier to buy clothes at home, Nanny. If I buy things in Paris they will either have to be made or fitted, and quite frankly I want to get back to the horses."

"Horses! Horses!" Nanny muttered as she pressed another heavy gown into the trunk. "What you should be thinking about is a husband and that is what his Lordship keeps on saying."

Malvina did not answer, as she did not want a long argument with Nanny as to whether she should marry the man her father wanted or continue to fight him as they had done before she had gone to Paris.

"I've put out that pretty pink gown for you to wear tonight," Nanny was saying. "And it's fortunate I brought the cape to go over it."

"It will do nicely," agreed Malvina.

She was wondering if the Duc would admire her in the dress – a very beautiful creation from Bond Street

Then she told herself once again it was something of no importance.

'I have to *stop* thinking about him,' she told herself.

She just knew that as far as she was concerned, the worst thing she could do at this precise moment was to go out to dinner with the Duc.

'But it will be something to remember when I am back in England,' she decided.

But it seemed to her that a jeering voice added,

'*And you will remember it just as you remembered his kiss.*'

Because Nanny wanted to button her up before she left for the theatre, Malvina changed very early.

It was in fact only seven o'clock when she walked down to the salon.

The theatre party had already left by the kitchen door.

The newspapers had come, but there did not seem to be anything particularly interesting in them.

She wondered if she would go into the library.

There was the cupboard full of newspaper cuttings about Cora Pearl – and then she told herself that she had no wish to read any more about the Parisian *courtesans*.

She had seen enough of them last night and while they might amuse men, they certainly did not amuse her.

She went to the nearest window and stood looking out at the small garden at the back of the house.

Now the shadows were growing longer and longer and soon the first stars would be twinkling in the sky.

She had a sudden longing to be down at the Seine as she was this afternoon with the Duc.

She wanted to hear him talking gently to her and at the same time watching the water in the river slipping past.

Again, however much she may try to forget, it was something she would always remember.

'I love him. I do love him,' she could not stop her heart repeating.

Then she felt ashamed of herself for being so weak.

Unexpectedly the door opened.

An old woman who Malvina reckoned must be the cook's sister peeped her head round.

"There be a lady to see you, mademoiselle."

Before Malvina had any chance to wonder who it could possibly be, Blanche came rushing into the room.

She was looking even more alluring than last night.

Glittering with sprays of jewels, she was wearing a spectacular gown in a soft spring green that matched the colour of her eyes.

Malvina moved towards her, but before she could say anything Blanche spoke out breathlessly,

"I am on my way to dinner, but I had to tell you, *ma chèrie*, what has just occurred."

"What has happened?" asked Malvina.

They were speaking in French and Blanche looked over her shoulder to make sure the door had been closed behind her and that no one was listening.

"I have just learnt from friends," she mouthed, "that Cora is leaving Charles."

"Leaving him! But why?"

"The Baron produced for her not only the bracelet she wanted but also a superb necklace that Oscar Mossin had designed especially for the President's wife, who had refused it because it was too expensive."

"So he has given it to Cora Pearl?"

"She grabbed at it with both hands!" cried Blanche, "but because she accepted it, Charles has walked out."

"Is he very upset?"

"He told my friend that she had left him without a franc in his pocket and a multitude of debts."

Blanche paused before she added,

"He then said, 'I suppose I shall have to go back to England and ask my father for the money to pay my debts, but he is determined to force me into marring some ghastly English girl who undoubtedly will bore me to tears'."

Malvine drew in her breath.

"Did he really say that?"

"That is just what he said to my friend," Blanche replied, "and I thought you ought to know."

"Thank you for telling me, it is very kind of you – "

Blanche bent to kiss her cheek.

"I must leave you now, *ma chèrie*, as the Prince is taking me out to dinner and we are then going on to a party afterwards. Although I doubt if it will be as amusing as mine!"

"I think that would be impossible, Blanche."

"You missed the best part, which was a very good thing. But at least you now know what Charles is like."

She turned towards the door and then she stopped.

"If you do end up marring him, you will find him very attractive and charming, as all Englishmen are. But you cannot expect him to be faithful!"

"No, I realise that and that is why I am determined not to marry him."

"There I think you are wise," agreed Blanche. "Of course, the best way to avoid it is to marry someone else. With your good looks you must have any number of men only too anxious to own you."

She did not wait for Malvina to answer, but pulled open the door and then she hurried across the hall.

Malvina followed her.

When they reached the front door, which was ajar, Blanche turned round and kissed Malvina.

"Goodnight, *ma chére*, come and see me tomorrow and I might have more news for you."

Again she did not wait for a reply, but hurried into her carriage where the Prince was waiting for her.

Malvina waved from the doorstep.

Only when the carriage was out of sight did she go inside and close the door.

Now, she pondered thoughtfully, things were even worse than they had been when she first came to Paris.

There was no doubt that the Marquis would try in every way possible to make Charles marry her.

Her father would undoubtedly still agree as he had before that it was an excellent marriage for both of them.

'What can I do?' Malvina asked herself.

Standing just inside the door where she had stood last night, she could feel the Duc's lips on hers.

*

Malvina was waiting patiently downstairs when the Duc arrived at exactly eight o'clock.

She had left the door of the salon open.

She could hear the carriage arriving outside before the footman either knocked on the door or rang the bell.

She thought it would be a mistake for the cook's cousin to tell Nanny who had called for her and that there had only been one gentleman doing so and no sign of her girlfriends.

The Duc stepped out to help her into the carriage.

Then as he joined her, he commented lightly,

"You are always punctual – and punctuality is most important but unusual in a woman."

"Now you are being unnecessarily rude," Malvina retorted. "I was taught when I was very young never to keep the horses waiting."

The Duc laughed.

"You are quite right in thinking that the horses are more important than anyone else."

Malvina gave a little cry.

"You are not wearing your sling!"

"I have been told there is no further need for it," the Duc explained. "But I have to be careful for a few days."

"Of course, and that means no riding."

The Duc smiled, but she knew it was something he was longing to resume.

They drove a little further before he remarked,

"I might be wrong, but I think this is the first time you have ever dined alone with a man."

"That is true, and I am sure that a proper English gentleman would not think of asking me to do so."

"Then it is a very good thing that I am an *improper* Frenchman. Because I can think of nothing more boring than if we had to always take a chaperone with us, being suspicious that there was a *double entendre* in everything we talked about!"

Malvina laughed as he had meant her to.

"We are going to a place where I often dine when I am alone," said the Duc. "You may find it dull, but at least we can talk without anyone listening or bothering us."

"That is an undoubted advantage," agreed Malvina.

The place he mentioned was only a short distance away and near to the Madeleine.

It was a small restaurant and there were alcoves at the back and along the sides of its walls.

Those sitting in these alcoves could hardly be seen by anyone except from the centre of the restaurant.

The Duc was obviously expected and they were led to an alcove at the far end of the room.

"To save time," he told her, "I have ordered what I think you will like, but, of course, we can change it if there is anything else you would prefer."

"I am perfectly prepared to bow to your superior judgement when it comes to food. I am afraid that at home we eat very English food, although it is well cooked and I try to order different menus every night."

"Now please tell me all about your family and how many there are of them," the Duc insisted.

"I think first," Malvina responded evasively, "you should tell me about your château. It is what you promised me and it would be terrible if we forgot it."

"I would not be likely to do so."

She had noticed that he carried something under his arm into the restaurant.

Now he opened the package and she saw an ancient engraving in colour.

For a moment it looked almost like a special cake of two tiers.

Then Malvina realised it was the painting of a large and beautifully proportioned château.

It was on a small island raised high above the moat which surrounded it and could only be reached by a bridge from the mainland.

The château itself was very different from anything she had ever seen as it consisted of what seemed a number of round towers topped by a pointed spire at each corner of the main building

As well as looking strong and well fortified it also looked very romantic.

The Duc put it into her hands and then waited.

"It is beautiful!" exclaimed Malvina. "I can quite understand why you want to restore it to the condition it was in before it was destroyed. Have you a picture of how it looks now?"

"If I had I could not bear to show it to you," the Duc sighed. "A little of the centre of the château remains, but the rounded towers have all lost their pointed tops.

"Of course, now there is no water in the moat and although the bridge to the mainland is still standing, it has no roof."

"You could put it all back," Malvina suggested to him gently.

"That is what I hope and believe. In the meantime I have to be content with my new château, which I admit is most comfortable and was constructed by my grandfather about seventy years ago."

He took the drawing from her.

"Now you know why I cannot spend a lot of time in Paris and why I cannot give you a necklace like the one you were wearing last night. Actually I think at your age the pearls you are wearing round your neck now are much more becoming."

A thought flashed through Malvina's mind.

If she had stayed with him last night as he expected her to do when they went to the pink room, he would have felt obliged to give her jewels of some sort.

Quickly she suggested,

"Don't let us talk about jewellery, which does not particularly interest me. But do tell me what you are really doing about your château. Is anyone working on it at the moment?"

"I have ten men, which is all I can afford, clearing away the rubble and finding out which walls would stand up to being added to if I can ever afford it."

"I am sure as it was a fortification, that will not be a problem, and I have thought of a way to help you find the money for restoration of your château, although you may think it either too childish or beneath your dignity."

"I promise to think of neither, Celeste."

"Well, as it was so famous as the *Palace of Kings*, there must be lots of people, not only in France, but from England and other countries of Europe who would come to visit your château if they knew that it was being restored to its former glory."

She saw that the Duc was listening and went on,

"After all you possess a glorious picture of what it originally looked like and that could be shown to tourists even before they came to France."

"I can see your point," the Duc responded a little doubtfully.

"Then when they see it, you get them to write their name on the bricks that you are repairing the château with and to give you the price of the brick itself, which would not be too many francs."

"Do you really think they would pay to have their names embedded in the château?"

"Why not?" replied Malvina. "I would think it very satisfying to know that the *Palace of Kings* in maybe seven years time enshrined my name and I am sure people from other lands would think it most romantic and rewarding."

The Duc did not respond, so she went on,

"Of course, what you must have for each of them is a replica of this picture so that they can take it home and show their friends where their name resides, and how they contributed towards the château being made as wonderful as it was before the Revolution."

She looked at him as she finished speaking to see if he approved of her ideas.

There was an expression in his eyes which for the moment she did not understand.

Then he said,

"I might have guessed that when I found you in the Madeleine immediately after I had prayed to St. Anthony, it was important I should do so. Of course, you are right and now I realise that I have been foolish in not thinking of some way the public could help me instead of trying to do everything myself."

"Anything so beautiful as your château must belong to the people of France," Malvina murmured softly.

The Duc raised his glass.

"I am now drinking a toast to you," he proposed, "because you are even more wonderful than you appeared to be when I first looked at you. You are an angel guiding me on the way to success – "

"Which I am quite certain you will have."

They talked on and on about the château, thinking of other ways they could coax in the public.

They laughed together at several ridiculous ideas that occurred to them in the course of their brainstorming, but were too outlandish to be treated seriously.

Suddenly they realised that there was no one left in the restaurant except themselves.

Malvina said somewhat reluctantly that she thought she ought to go home.

"Is anyone waiting up for you?" the Duc enquired.

She told him then how she had sent Nanny with the other servants in the house to the theatre.

"It is something Nanny will always remember when we get back to London," she added.

"She will have returned by this time, and therefore I must take you back. I realise I must be so careful of your reputation. But may I add I have *never* enjoyed an evening more."

Malvina knew that she could say the same.

Yet somehow the words would not escape her lips.

"Tomorrow," he suggested, "I want to take you on a boat down the Seine. There is a little place about an hour away where we can take luncheon, which I think you will enjoy and which will be very different from anywhere you have been before."

Malvina did not say that she was leaving tomorrow morning.

She thought he might try to persuade her to stay a bit longer.

She recognised that if he did so, it would only make what she was feeling worse.

She loved him – because she could not help it.

It would be sheer agony in a day or two to have to go back to England and never to see him again.

She was well aware that all the aristocratic families in France had arranged marriages.

It was only surprising, as he was twenty-seven, that the Duc had not been married already.

She was quite certain his relatives were beseeching him to marry someone suitable, someone whose blood was as blue as his and theirs.

'To him,' she reflected, 'I am just an English girl of no particular consequence who can dine with him without a chaperone and who could become involved with someone like Blanche d'Antigny and be dressed up by her to attend one of her improper parties.'

She glanced at the Duc and continued with her deep thoughts,

'He finds me amusing and likes talking to me, but that is not love and not what I am feeling about *him*.'

The Duc was paying the bill.

Malvina hoped that it was not more than he could afford, but the food had certainly been delicious.

When they walked outside his carriage was waiting.

He gave the order without her speaking to return to the *Faubourg St. Honoré*.

As they drove off, he turned to Malvina,

"Have you enjoyed the evening?"

"It has been wonderful, thank you very, very much. And of course I shall long to know if our ideas for your château ever work out."

"I am making more plans and it is something we will talk about tomorrow. First of all I want you to join me for luncheon and we will go down the Seine about eleven o'clock. In the evening I will take you to another place for dinner which will be a secret until we arrive there."

"It all sounds wonderful. Are you quite certain you have not anything more important to do?"

"I can think of nothing more important than being with you!"

There was a note in his voice which made her feel as if once again he was kissing her.

It was almost a feeling of relief when the horses came to a standstill in front of the house.

"I expect you have your key with you," the Duc asked, putting out his hand.

Malvina gave him the key and he stepped out.

He turned the key in the lock and the door opened.

Perhaps it was Nanny or the cook's cousin who had left a small oil lamp burning in the hall.

The door of the salon was open to reveal another lamp alight in there.

Malvina stood still just as she had last night to say goodnight to the Duc.

To her surprise he closed the door.

She said quickly,

"I am afraid I have no nightcap to offer you. I did not think of asking the servants for one."

The Duc did not answer.

She saw he was looking to where under the stairs one of her trunks had been brought down to the hall.

It was ready for her to leave the next day.

Malvina walked swiftly into the salon and the Duc followed her.

"Why is that trunk in the hall?" he now demanded. "When are you leaving?"

He spoke sharply and for some reason she could not lie to him.

"I am going back to England – tomorrow morning."

"In which case I shall be coming with you – to meet your father."

"To meet my father? But why?"

There was a pause.

Then the Duc added, surprisingly in French,

"I wish to ask him to grant me the honour of your hand in marriage."

CHAPTER SEVEN

For a moment Malvina could only stare at him.

Then she asked in a voice he could hardly hear,

"What are you – *saying*? What are you – *asking*?"

"I am asking you to be my wife."

"But how can you? You know nothing about me."

The Duc smiled tenderly at her.

"I know everything that I do need to know. I knew from the first moment I saw you that I had to make you mine. Now I realise I want much more than that. I want you with me as my wife and there will be no question of any other man kissing you but me."

Just as he finished speaking, he put his arms around Malvina and his lips were on hers.

At first he kissed her gently.

Then more possessively.

She felt the rapture she had not understood before sweep through her body until it consumed her.

The Duc kissed her and went on kissing her till they were both breathless.

When he raised his head, he said in a voice which was deep and strange,

"I love you. I love you as I have always wanted to love someone but thought I never would."

"Can it really be true?" she asked.

"It is true, my darling, and we will be married as soon as I have secured your father's consent."

He drew her a little closer.

"There may be difficulties perhaps from my family. But nothing matters except that I love you and I found you when I feared love would never happen to me."

He looked down at her so tenderly before he asked,

"And do you love me?"

"I love you. I do love you," sighed Malvina. "And I was running away from you, because I thought you would never love me."

"How could you think anything so foolish? I was wooing you gently because I was afraid of frightening you. But I have loved you from the very first moment when you sat beside me at dinner.

"Then when I took you upstairs, I tried to pretend it was an ordinary casual affair. But I knew when I took you home that you were mine and I could never lose you."

Malvina gave a small cry and hid her face against his shoulder.

"I think I am dreaming. That is what I too wanted, but thought I would never have."

"We will be very happy," the Duc assured her. "I have been pushed and pleaded with ever since I left Oxford to marry someone very suitable as is to be expected of any Frenchman in my position."

"But how can you think I am suitable?"

"You are what I want and what I intend to have. As I say, there may be difficulties, my darling one, perhaps not only with my family in France but with yours in England. But as long as we are together, nothing will matter as long as we have each other."

The way he spoke made Malvina feel she wanted to cry with sheer happiness.

How was it possible after all she had felt about him that the Duc really loved her as she wanted to be loved?

"I must now tell you all about myself. You cannot marry me without knowing who I am."

"It does not matter *who* you are, my darling. You will have my name as soon as the ring is on your finger!"

He looked down at her with an expression of love in his eyes.

For the moment Malvina seemed to forget all they were saying.

She sensed that her whole body was now vibrating towards him.

When he kissed her, the rapture of his kiss carried her up into the sky.

"I love you," she murmured because she could not help it.

"And I love you, my darling, more than I can ever put into words."

As he spoke he pulled her down onto the sofa.

Then he kissed her again and again until she put out her hands and pressed them against his chest.

"You must listen to me. I must explain to you what has happened."

"What has happened – is that I have fallen in love with the most beautiful girl I have ever seen in my life. If she loves me, then I know that the gates of Heaven are open and this time I shall not be left outside."

Because she knew just what he was referring to, she blushed.

"You will have to forget that, and our families must never know that we met at Blanche's dinner party."

"My family would be absolutely horrified," agreed the Duc, "and I suspect yours would be too. But you *must* tell me why you were there."

"That is exactly what I am trying to do!"

"I think perhaps," the Duc now interrupted, "that I should tell you first about my mother's family in England, as they will naturally be concerned that I am marrying an English girl. As I have told you, my mother was English."

"That is exactly why you looked so different from all the other men at the party."

"It is the sort of party that I shall never allow you to attend, and I promise you I will never again be a guest."

He paused for a moment.

"You are far too beautiful. I am going to take you well away from Paris. If I don't, I feel I shall be fighting a thousand duels to keep other men away from you."

"I want no one but you – now and for ever. It was because I was afraid of being married that I came to Paris."

"Thank God you did so."

He kissed her again ardently so it was impossible for her to speak.

When he raised his head, he said,

"I was going to tell you more about my family in England. My mother was the third daughter of the Duke of Berlington. I stayed with them while I was at Oxford and they tried to marry me off to one English girl after another as soon as I had finished my studies there."

"The Duke of Berlington!" exclaimed Malvina. "I know the Duke. He has been to see my father's horses."

"The present Duke is my uncle. But why was he seeing your father's horses?"

"Because he admired them so and one of them had won the Derby last year."

"Your father's horse?"

There was an obvious note of surprise in his voice.

"I am still trying to tell you who I am, but you are making it rather difficult – "

"That is one thing I have no wish to do, my darling, but I do not want you to feel hurt if my family in England or France does not welcome you with open arms. They have chosen a dozen aristocratic brides for me and been so furious when I refused to even meet them and I now realise that I was really waiting for *you*."

"And now you have found me," she murmured.

"Just like a fairy story, my darling, and we will live together happily ever after for Eternity. Whatever anyone feels about our marriage will not concern us."

Malvina realised by the way he was speaking that he was afraid they would be upset at his choice of bride.

She recognised that if they knew how they had met, that was only to be expected.

Again she felt a wave of happiness flood over her.

The Duc was determined to marry her despite the opposition he might well expect.

Softly she suggested,

"I think you are worrying unnecessarily. I am sure your uncle who was so enthusiastic about my Papa's horses will be more than happy for you to marry me. The only objection your French family could make to our marriage is that I am English instead of being French."

The Duc's lips had been moving gently over her forehead while she spoke.

She had the feeling he was not listening to what she was saying.

Then as if he was suddenly aware she was waiting for his answer, he enquired a little sharply,

"Perhaps we should make a start by you telling me your real name."

"It is Malvina – " she began.

"To me you will always have to be Celeste because the name means 'heavenly,' and that, my lovely angel, is what you are."

He kissed her before she could reply.

"I love you," Malvina whispered to him when she could speak.

"And I adore and worship you, my little angel."

His lips sought hers again.

Some time later Malvina tried again,

"Please, darling, listen. I am Malvina Silisley, and my father is the fifth Earl of Silstone."

She felt the Earl stiffen and then he stared at her.

"Lord Silstone!" he exclaimed. "Of course, I have heard of his horses. He not only won the Derby last year but also the Oaks."

"Papa will be so delighted you know so much about him."

"If you are really Lord Silstone's daughter, and I do believe you, how on earth could you possibly be disguised as a *cocotte* at Blanche's dinner party?

He sounded so astonished that Malvina could only laugh.

"It does sound fantastic," she agreed, "but Papa told me that he had arranged for me to marry Charles Arram."

The Duc gasped.

"So you then came to Paris to see what Charles was like?"

"How clever of you to guess. That is exactly what I did. I went to see Blanche because one of the girls I was at school with had been told about her by her brother. She understood exactly why I wanted to see Charles when he was off his guard and not aware that anyone connected with England was watching him."

"You certainly got what you came for," laughed the Duc.

"I was going back to England to tell my Papa that it is totally impossible for me to marry someone who was enamoured of Cora Pearl. Then this evening, before you arrived for me, Blanche came in to tell me that Charles has quarrelled with Cora over the Baron and is going to return to England because he has run out of money."

"Are you now telling me in a somewhat roundabout fashion that it is your money he really desires?"

"It is really his father who wants it," she explained, "and he and Papa arranged it all between them that I should marry Charles. Papa is so positive about the idea because he wants to link our estates together as they are adjoining. But when he suddenly left for Scotland on business, I was determined to come to Paris and find some way of saving myself."

She spoke in a manner that told the Duc just how frightened she had been.

"Now you have found me, Malvina, and I promise you I will not let you marry anyone else."

"It is so wonderful and I cannot believe it is true. Now I can help you with your château and actually it will thrill Papa to help you as well. It is just the sort of project that interests him, and it will make up to him for losing the Marquis's estate next door."

"What you are now saying makes me feel, if I am sensible, that I should marry you before going to England. Are you quite certain, my lovely darling, that your father will not refuse to let you marry me and insist that Charles is your bridegroom?"

"Papa does want me to be happy and as he loved my mother very deeply, I know he will realise how much I love you."

The Duc's arms tightened round her, but before he could kiss her, she added,

"I am sure too that he will be very delighted you are related to the Duke of Berlington. They compete in almost every big race and it will be amusing to know there is some connection with the Duke who he has managed to outrace quite a number of times."

The Duc laughed.

"So horses come into it even when it concerns us!"

"Of course they do and just as Papa has some of the best racehorses in England, we must have the best horses in France."

She saw the light in the Duc's eyes and knew it was something he wanted himself.

Then he said,

"I know you are telling me that you are rich. But I swear to you on everything I hold holy that I would marry you if you did not own a centime and your father had not even a four-legged donkey."

Malvina laughed.

"I know that, and it is so wonderful, so utterly and so completely wonderful, that you do love me and that you wanted to marry me without even knowing who I was."

"How could I help it, Malvina or Celeste? You are already a part of me and I can read your thoughts as you can read mine. I know when I kiss you it is the kiss of love which I have always longed for, but never found in anyone else."

"I shall be very jealous if you find it anywhere else in the future!"

"Not half as jealous as I shall feel about you, my darling. You are far too beautiful not to attract every man you meet. I think the best thing I can do is to lock you away in my château and you will see no one except me!"

Malvina laughed again.

"I don't think I would mind, but it might be just a little uncomfortable for our children, if we have any."

The Duc held her even closer.

"Of course we will have children. I was an only child and very lonely."

"So was I," admitted Malvina.

"There are a million things we have in common and it is going to take the rest of our lives to talk about them."

He looked down at her lovingly.

"That is, when you are able to talk because I am not kissing you!"

Then he was kissing her again.

Kissing her till Malvina felt they had been swept up into the sky and were touching the stars.

They had found, as the Duc had said, that the gates of Heaven were open.

When they went in through them they were part of the real love which all men and women seek but only a few are privileged to find.

The Love which comes only from God and to find it is to be in Heaven.